Old Buddy Old Pal

Old Buddy Old Pal

by

Michael Laser

THE PERMANENT PRESS
SAG HARBOR, NY 11963

Copyright© 1999 by Michael Laser

Library of Congress Cataloging-in-Publication Data

Laser, Michael
    Old Buddy Old Pal / byMichael Laser
      p. cm.
    ISBN 1-57962-021-3
    I. Title.

813'.54--dc21　　　　　　　　　　　98-34209
　　　　　　　　　　　　　　　　　　　CIP

All rights reserved, including the right to reproduce this book, or parts thereof, in any form, except for the inclusion of brief quotes in a review

THE PERMANENT PRESS
4170 Noyac Road
Sag Harbor, NY 11963

For my mother, who created this ambition,
and for Mr. Catania, who nourished it.

Acknowledgments

Many friends, acquaintances and strangers helped me by generously answering questions or allowing me to observe them at work. They include: Marshall Schoen, Janice Castle, Andrea Levin, Jim Henshaw, Keith Hicks, Mindy Birnbaum, Michael Giaquinto, Dr. Michael Flynn, Isadora Silverman, Ira Cure, Anita Winkler, Dr. Brian Levy, Dr. Kevin Crutchfield, Joe Bleshman, and Dr. Adam Silvers. My wife, Jennifer Prost, read what I thought was a final draft and made helpful comments. The Telephone Reference Service of the N.Y. Public Library has answered so many questions over the years that I have come to love and depend on it like a member of my family. Finally, I would like to thank the staff of the Andrew Heiskell Library for the Blind and Physically Handicapped in Manhattan, who welcomed me during lunch hours even though I'm not blind or physically handicapped.

A friend to me is someone that cares for me as much as I care for them. A friend is a person that tells me what I need to hear and not what I want to hear. Also a friend is a person I can share all my deep dark secrets with no matter what happens. They will be there through good and bad times. I want someone to respect me just for me and not expect anything else out of me. Someone who can confide in me about their feelings and thoughts.

Well I haven't found one yet.

—from a collection of writings by adult literacy students at The Fortune Society

1.

A GOOD HOT night, with a breeze. Streets full of women, tan legs and some nice bare shoulders. A relief to have plans tonight after four evenings alone. And even if it's just the same-as-always walk with Alan, down Broadway and over the Brooklyn Bridge, the city always supplies at least one bizarre and entertaining incident.

Smell of ink reaches past the locked lobby doors of Alan's building—the same one where my uncle used to run a printing shop. Someday, when he owns fifty apartment houses and the Plaza Hotel, Alan will drive by here with his kids and show them the humble, sooty origins of the empire. (I forgive him his mercenary ambitions because there's no greed in him, only a compulsion to fulfill his father's dreams.)

Have to admit, it impresses me to see his name in the intercom directory, the small white letters fitted into the black felt grooves, an *Inc.* above, a *Co.* below. Not just a person—a profit-making enterprise.

Blizzard of intercom noise, can't hear what he said. Doesn't buzz me in, so he must be on his way down. Quick reflection-check in the scratched glass door, make sure nothing moronic is going on in my appearance. Hair bunched somewhat on one side, knead it a bit, redistribute the wealth.

Here he comes, out of the elevator. Charcoal gray suit, black briefcase, i.e., meeting with the bank today. Used to be, he walked leaning forward 10 degrees, energetically, as if he couldn't wait to meet the future. He still walks with a lean, but now he just looks tired.

The scar on the back of his hand climbs up his shirt-cuff, a white serpent. Strong business handshake and an affectionate but distracted "B-man!" He's been calling me this for a decade, since freshman year, and it always sends a little zip of pleasure up the back of my neck. No one else ever gave me a nickname—and with the name Burt, you crave one.

We head east, as always.

"How'd you do at the bank?"

"What bank?"

"I assumed from the suit."

"I was in Housing Court all day."

"Ah. Your favorite place."

Disgusted: "As soon as they hear the word 'Brooklyn,' they assume you're a slumlord."

He doesn't realize he's said this before, verbatim.

"What was it about?"

"A guy with a dead cat. It's pathetic, he says I'm putting lead in his water to get him out. The lawyer belongs in jail for taking his money. I wanted to punch her in the teeth."

Most likely the facts are as he says. Lurking suspicions, though, because he's a landlord and I come from a long line of tenants.

"What about the new renovation, how's it going?"

"Great."

Bad sign. *Great*, from Alan, means concealed problems. It's not our way for me to challenge, though. He doesn't want me to. Believe me.

At his suggestion, we turn downtown on Sixth instead of Broadway. The Flower District: potted trees and plants take up most of the sidewalk, seven-foot plumes dyed in gaudy colors bend over us languorously, like a rajah's punkah. A sidewalk belt-and-purse merchant from somewhere in Africa haggles with two Chinese girls who can't stop laughing. Pair of black kids give each other a hard time, "You fucked up," "No *you* fucked up," then quiet down as they cross through a small battalion of chunky white guys and gals, look like hockey fans en route to a Rangers game except it's the wrong season. "Vin, stop teasing huh," whines a gal with a beer in a brown bag.

My cosmopolis.

"*Mira,*" murmurs Alan.

Miniskirt, straight black hair, an unsmiling Spanish

Pocahontas with cheekbones that could put a nasty gash in any man's confidence. Lit cigarette between long bony fingers. Her eyes touch mine, then swing away like a tank's gun-barrel.

I give a puppy-whimper when she's past, and Alan snickers. We've been doing this since college. He (married now, engaged then, though not to Lori) points them out, and I (almost always between girlfriends) turn my suffering lust into comedy.

Distracted, I nearly plant my foot on a wet wad of something, but with a lightning jig I evade the gross blob. Alan laughs out loud, which doesn't please me, but I guess it did look comical.

Past the white cast-iron fortresses that were department stores in the time of our great-grandparents. Fluted columns, endless narrow windows. Alan talked about buying one of these buildings once, in partnership with two relatives, but couldn't get the price he wanted. He knows about money, knows what's a good deal and what isn't. If it weren't such a kid-brotherish thing to do, I would ask him to teach me the hidden knowledge of his trade: the semilicit ploys that make profit possible, the maneuverings my father, the socialist high school teacher, despised without ever knowing. How to offer a bribe to a building inspector when you think he wants one but can't tell for sure. How to get the tenants out of a building so you can renovate, without hiring armed thugs. Not that I would ever use the information, but it's always good to decrease one's ignorance.

He's staring at the sky's last light, or else at that lamppost, at the rust-stained platter that commemorates Honduras, one of the Americas that this is the Avenue of. "Have you ever heard anyone actually say, 'Avenue of the Americas'?" I ask. "As opposed to 'Sixth Avenue'?"

A passing train blows hot stale air through a sidewalk grate. Empty matchbook flutters up like a butterfly. I don't think he heard me.

Past Ray's Pizza, the one all the others stole the name from, and where Crazy Eddie used to be. Cross the avenue, and down past the sidewalk entrepreneurs, each with a different shade of skin—black incense-sellers in Islamic white, red-nosed vendor of old paperbacks displayed shingle-style on the concrete, multi-crucifix guy with salsa on his boom box and old *Life* magazines stacked high on a bridge table—until we come to the playground basketball game across from the Waverly. "Want to spectate?"

He checks his watch, *Lori, supper*, but nods. A young mom pulls her twitchy red-headed boy and shopping cart aside to make room for us at the chain-link fence. Inside, ten black guys shout, wave, hurl passes and shoot. Small one in a green sweatband controls the ball carefully, dribbling low. A willful drive to the basket, churning his way through the defenders, then he takes off, bony ankles flying, neck-veins standing out, one sneaker hits someone in the leg, and the layup, yes!

"Nice, right?"

Alan's unimpressed. "Showboating," he says. "He should've passed."

Yet the little guy's aggression reminds me exactly of Alan on the basketball court. I watched him play one-on-one a couple times at college: a shock, to see my generous, empathetic friend turn into a jock, someone who *wanted to win*. Not a mode that's available to me.

Barechested guy with dreadlocks grabs a rebound and flings it downcourt, no bounce, so hard that his man can't hold onto it. "I got to put it in your weak hands for you?" he screams, a Jamaican Ralph Kramden bellowing at a scrawny Norton with a shaved head. How do guys stay friends after that? I couldn't. Hard to believe any real-life Norton could, except with gallons of swallowed rage. It's just a convention of TV, that friends hold no grudges, have no memories.

The redheaded kid with his mother—something's wrong with him, his head jerks from side to side, his fingers clutch the fence, and now he squeals, "Swish!" though no ball has gone through the hoop and there is no net. Tall and skinny, thirteen or so, too big to sound like that. The mother's only a few years older than Alan and me, an appealing smart face, but weary. "Jamie, ssh."

Another squeal, "I'm gonna slam dunk it!" then someone mimics him: mean white teen further down the fence, no shirt or chest hair, two sets of untied laces in his boot-sized sneakers. He's got a chuckling buddy for an audience, a worm. Each with the brown lip of a beer bottle peeking out of a brown bag.

Jamie tries again, "I'm gonna slam dunk it!" and the prick mimics him again.

I'd like to kill him. Or just put a gun in his mouth and scare the hell out of him, so he'd never speak in public again.

The mother tells Jamie it's time to go, the ice cream is melting.

"I want to watch the *game*," Jamie whines.

"I want to watch the *game*," whines Vicious.

I could go talk to him, offer to break his nose. There would be backtalk, though, and since I'm not the punch-throwing type, it would soon turn to quicksand.

"Hey Jamie," Alan says, "what's your favorite team?"

The boy is uncertain, can't tell who's friend and who's foe, so he blares his answer defensively, "The Knicks!"

Alan asks what players Jamie likes, and Jamie names some people I've never heard of, not being a fan. The delinquent duo turn back to the game and glug their beer.

Mom gives us a soft look, as if touched that anyone could be so decent in this gone-to-shit world. Alan asks Jamie, "How'd you like Starks' alley-oop to Ewing in that last game?" and the boy leaps straight up and slaps the fence. His mother smooths his hair with her hand.

Victory, relief: the two pustules leave and descend into the subway. *This* is what Alan was put on earth to do, not to acquire buildings. But you can't make a living defending the weak.

He checks his watch again, and so do I. Time to move on, Kemo Sabe.

The mother says a quiet, direct "Thanks," and we head south. I nudge Alan in the arm, "What a guy."

"No, they made me sick."

He's taking off into the clouds again, leaving me for other thoughts. This time I grab him before he gets away.

"You seem preoccupied tonight."

"Sorry. I guess I am."

"About what?"

"The coffee shop in my Fulton Street building is going out of business. That's seven thousand a month I'll be losing until I get a new tenant."

Not the kind of problem I'm good at solving. "What'll you do, put an ad in the paper?"

"Or else try to flip the building. I took it with a balloon mortgage and the balloon comes due in a few months. One thing after another."

I'm not sure what a balloon mortgage is, or how you flip a building if you're not Superman. Too proud to ask, I can't find another word to say, can only remember the building itself. Dirty tan bricks, shirts hanging out of the upper windows, a depressing place, like all of his properties.

We swing east on Bleecker Street, a film between us.

•

It's no great mystery why we've drifted apart. Ten years ago, we slept in the same room and ate at the same table every day. Now you could draw a line down a page and list the ways we're different. Married/single. Landlord/literacy worker. Leather briefcase/canvas knapsack. Our lives have diverged like the branching smoke-trails of the *Challenger* explosion.

We keep quiet about this (I can't imagine speaking the simple truth, "Looks like we don't have much in common any more") but it hangs between us, always. While I frequent smelly guitar bars like Ruff City, he and Lori pack champagne in a picnic basket and go hear Philharmonic in the Park. While I seek out foreign and low-budget movies that never play west of the Hudson, they buy season tickets to the ballet. And it goes beyond style. His run-ins with tenants have soured him on poor people, though he watches what he says in deference to my politics. Meanwhile I, who never stopped believing that housing should have nothing to do with profit, have learned to suspend judgment, to give him credit for providing clean lobbies and halls in low-income neighborhoods, to look not directly at his business but just to the side of it.

No wonder we can't talk.

Our walks used to be better. He would come up with questions from left field and coax new thoughts out of me, while we bought bananas at a Hasidic fruit stand in Williamsburg, watched a Mets game in an Irish bar in Inwood, took tastes of Polish sausage at a Greenpoint meat market. The idea was to roam the city and *talk* to each other, instead of sitting together facing a TV like other guys. "What was the point of that experiment with the dead frogs and the electricity?" he asked one time. I didn't know, but I knew the scientist's name was Galvani and *galvanizing* comes from his name, so then we played with the idea of bringing frogs back to life with electric shock and storing them in galvanized garbage cans. That led to an appreciation of doctors for the indisputable usefulness of their work, and from there to the opposite end of the spectrum, the lifeless and/or surly civil servant, and the corruption scandal at the Parking Violations Bureau, and my theory about parking meters, that since all those coins can't possibly fit inside the small gray meter-heads, the poles must really be conduits to underground pipes that suck the money downtown, and with a pickaxe you could siphon off a substantial income. I think that was the same night we debated the morality of the death penalty.

Those walks shine in memory—but the fact is, even they were a step down from our Adventure Nights. Right after college, when we'd just moved back to the city, we used to take turns leading each other into unusual experiences. Flying over the Empire State Building in a helicopter, firing .38 Specials at a basement pistol range, listening to a lamp repairman argue with a customer in small claims court. I started the whole thing, as a way to hoist his spirits after his catastrophic breakup that spring. Once he revived, though, it turned into a contest: who could come up with the weirdest activity. After a while, new adventures got harder to find, and we veered into the ridiculous. (An introductory tap-dancing lesson, Bingo night at a church in Little Italy, personality-evaluation by scientologists.) He liked to embarrass me wherever we went, as a joke, like at the Bingo church, lying to an old woman in black that I spoke Italian and wanted to practice but was shy. In return, I punched him in the arm, though to be honest I kind of enjoyed it, just like I enjoy him calling me *B-Man*. Then I made the mistake of trying to turn the tables and embarrass *him*, by taking him to a topless bar. That was the last of our Adventure Nights.

I knew I'd blundered the second we walked in. Not that it was a vile pit—the room seemed clean enough, with red and blue lights and wall-to-wall mirrors. It was just the dreary quiet of the men, watching the flat-chested woman dance lazily across the platform behind the bar, while she watched her reflection behind us. Alan kidded me, "You're *sure* you've never been here before?" but that was only his way of going easy on me. We watched the dancer inertly and drank our drinks, while an obese monster in thick glasses growled, "Yeah!" every minute or two, as if to say, Woho, this is hot!

The dancer stopped in front of us, folded her arms, and flexed a muscle so that one breast jumped. Before I could find the words to get us out the door, an adorable blond girl in a leopardskin bikini and glasses slipped between our stools and leaned back against the bar. It was winter, we still had on sweaters and coats, but here was this milk-white skin inches from our hands. "Bet ya girlfriends don't know ya here," she said, friendly but keeping an eye on someone near the door.

Alan got me back. He said we were Bible salesmen from Idaho, and that I'd just broken up with my sweetheart and needed cheering up. She asked me who broke up with who and other sympathetic questions. I stumbled and fumbled, "It wasn't anything serious, no big deal," until she put her arm around my shoulder and said she used to love reading the Bible and couldn't understand atheists. Who did they think made the mountains and the sky?

While I froze at her touch—to have almost the thing you crave, but not really, not at all—Alan stared at her pale smooth shoulder, so hard that it worried me. He hadn't gone out with anyone since the spring before, and I wasn't sure what he might be willing to do.

The scare didn't last, though. She said she'd love to spend some time with us, we looked nice, but someone had to buy her a drink. That burst the bubble. We left, and the next week Alan said, Why don't we just go to a hockey game? The week after that I said, How about a long walk?

I don't often look back like this, but since I've come this far, might as well go all the way: to college, when he used to keep me up into the middle of the night talking across the dark room, and pry me away from studying to throw a football around behind the dorm, and hug my waist in front of our friends while I squirmed away and laughed.

And then ten years went by, and that luminous Alan turned into the drab, distracted landlord beside me.

•

If we were cops, risking our lives together, each holding himself responsible for the other's survival, then everything would be different. We could talk about any nonsense at all and never worry about the health of our friendship, because the small talk would only be a cover for the fierce mutual loyalty underneath. As it is, we face no physical dangers, and have little to bind us except habit and the fear of friendlessness.

So, would I rather we were cops?

Yes, I would.

•

The sky has gone to orange smoke behind the towers of downtown. A ferry swims away from its dock like a big beetle riding the silver-blue water. Above the World Trade Center, a sliver of moon rests on its back. Soaring webwork cables, heavy brown stones, gothic arches: this bridge has always reminded me of a cathedral. A sacred place, because my father used to cross it every day on his way to the school where he taught.

Somewhere along here, a cable once snapped and killed a guy. Feet hot inside shoes, breeze-dried sweat cooling my forehead. We're too tired to talk over the noise of traffic below, but also have nothing to say.

A pair of small old men point cameras at the skyline, prospecting for beauty. Lean runner lopes by, juggling four tangerines. "Haven't seen him in a while," I venture.

"That's not him, that's a new one."

I smirk. Alan smiles too.

"Pretty night," I say.

He glances out at the harbor, then his focus shifts to the nearer distance, to nothing in particular. A seagull glides by three feet above our heads. Whatever he's thinking, it has nothing to do with me or this bridge.

Why do you always fade away like this? What's with you?

Legitimate questions, but not askable. Time to face the possibility that we've used this friendship up.

•

Dark and dignified, his brownstone sits snug between two neighbors just like it. Each of the three has a bay window on the first floor and stone steps leading to a door of oak and beveled glass. You can see the Statue of Liberty from his roof, but he only took me there once, because walking on the tarpaper compromises the waterproofing. His words, not mine.

They inherited this house from Lori's childless uncle,

who made his fortune manufacturing some kind of screw for the Navy. First time I saw it, my stomach sank. Another difference between us. Another wedge.

Through the black iron gate and down two steps to the humble ground floor entrance. The smell of Lori's Luscious Meat Sauce comes out to greet us through the open window. Something to look forward to: Lori's company, and her cooking. Usually she broils a steak from her father's butcher shop, but personally I prefer this thick, democratic spaghetti sauce with bits of onion and slivers of green pepper. Comfort as opposed to luxury.

"I'm ho-ome," I sing.

"Oh, and you brought company," says she, coming out of the kitchen with a wooden spoon in her hand, smear of dandelion-yellow paint on her jeans. Gives us each a kiss, barely a difference between the two kisses, which is flattering. Clean coconut fragrance of her shampoo mixes with the sauce aroma, and now that we're inside I can smell her oil paints too. So many of life's pleasures come through the nose.

Alan goes up to change, Lori leads me into the living room. Glass, leather and chrome furniture, a doctor's waiting room—Alan's inexplicable taste, softened a bit by Lori's plants. Easel set up near the front windows, bowl of lemons on windowsill, wind-up alarm clock alongside. She has rendered the objects realistically on canvas, with this addition: in the painting, an old woman has stopped in a fictional garden just outside the window, startled, and is peeking in. A dreamy image, like all of her paintings. (She also paints watercolor illustrations for children's books—she does the *Ned the Neck* series, about a clumsy giraffe who lives in Manhattan—but those cute, lucrative pictures come from a different part of her.)

"Don't look so closely," she says, "you'll see the problems."

"If you're not going to hang this one up, will you give it to me?"

"Now now" is all she says. Despite my prodding, she

never displays her paintings or tries to sell them. They just pile up in the basement, and it drives me crazy.
"Can I get you something to drink? We have that sour cherry juice you like."
"Just a glass of water."
She goes back to the kitchen. Let her play hostess if that's what she wants, I've given up trying to pry candor out of her. Pick up a couple of wrinkled Winsor & Newton tubes, Burnt Sienna, Cerulean Blue. She strews a thick handful of dry spaghetti, color of Brueghel hay, around the inside of a big pot. Familiar sight: Lori's slender back as she works at the stove.

Returning, she hands me a deep blue tumbler with floating ice and an arc of lime straddling the lip. My fingers brush against her bone-thin wrist, and leaping desire latches onto the pale, freckled arms exposed by her sleeveless shirt.

Let's get this out of the way: long ago, just after college, I was in love with her, but couldn't believe she would go out with me, dwelling as she did on a higher plane. We met in a life-drawing class; her pencil sketches made mine look thick and cloddish. So, despite the warm bath of acceptance in her eyes, I kept putting off The Kiss, the lover's gambling leap. The longer it dragged on, the more I elevated her in my mind. "Are you the perfect person?" I actually asked her once—but never did kiss her, not even when she came over and sat on my lap in my own easy chair, smiling bravely at me, because even then I couldn't be sure it meant what it seemed to, and what if I kissed her and that *wasn't* what she wanted? (Fool, idiot, coward.) I might have eventually made a move, but I neglected to tell Alan about her, and when he met her at my birthday party, he talked to no one else and that was that. Couldn't bear to see either of them for a few weeks, but the pain passed. By the time they got married, I saw all the reasons why we would have failed as a couple: 1) she never reveals anything about herself, 2) she has no political beliefs whatsoever, and 3) she never showed her teeth when she smiled at me, whereas with Alan they flashed from that first night on. (Snowball fight in

Central Park, glinting white snow, glinting white incisors, the two of them happy as lovers in a toothpaste commercial.) Just after the wedding, when she cut off most of her chestnut hair, the finest, softest hair I've ever seen, I regretted never having touched it, but felt somewhat less bereft.

She joins me on the hard leather couch, barely making a dent in it. On the glass coffee table, a Sunday *Times* magazine beneath a small pile of mail. Letters from Citibank and Chase addressed to Alan, first class, not bulk mail. Replies to loan applications?

"You look back to normal," she says. "Are you recovered?"

Huh? Oh right, she means from my breakup, a month ago, with a woman I only dated for three weeks. Embarrassing, that there's always a different woman, a different breakup to report.

"I'm fine. Ready to take on the next contender."

"You're so good at bouncing back."

Wide thin mouth tipped up at the corners, and that warm steady gaze that always makes my eyes sneak away. So much fondness—*What does she want,* I used to ask myself after Alan married her and she kept looking at me this way. By now I understand that she doesn't want anything, just likes me, sees I'm lonely, wishes I could find a mate. Which makes it not entirely comfortable to be around her.

Here comes Alan, in cut-offs and yellowed gym shirt from college. Plops next to Lori, hand on her knee, then bounces forward to the edge of the couch to sort through the mail. She hooks a pinky through one of his belt-loops and briefs him on the day's business. His father wants him to call back about Saturday; the mechanic said it's the voltage regulator, should have the car ready by tomorrow; and her sister-in-law has to have a cyst removed. Alan nodding and frowning, as appropriate, while he flips through envelopes. The mystery of marriage: is this a good one, with its mild affection and divided attention? Is this the best one can hope for? And if so, does marriage warrant all my bachelor envy and grief?

She goes back to the kitchen, stirs the spaghetti, removes a hunk of Parmesan cheese from the gigantic refrigerator. Alan opens his mail with a brass blade while a neighbor's dog yaps frenziedly. "I'm going to shoot that dog someday," he says as Lori returns, sits, rests her hand on his back.

What a friend I am. They include me in their evening as generously as if I were a third spouse, while I sit in judgment on their marriage and their furnishings. (That pastel poster, Southwest landscape stylized down to a few salmon curves and gray horizontals: market research art. While her paintings go unseen!)

"Ugly's getting married," Alan says. Cream-colored invitation in his hand, scalloped edges, a note on the back.

First reaction, honestly? *He found someone before I did.*

"Look at this. He's doing it in Gold River."

Our college town. He hands me the invitation, lacy script, triple-embossed border. Mr. and Mrs. Greene, Mr. and Mrs. Horowitz, honor of your presence, their children Deborah Dawn and Gerald Harvey, Holiday Inn, Gold River, New York.

"Wonder if I'm invited." Hoping not. He was such a jerk.

On the back, in big messy letters, *It'll be a reunion—football on the quad. No blackhead-squeezing allowed! Gerry.*

A snort pops out of me. I'd forgotten Alan's famous skin problems. He used to lean into the mirror in our corridor's only bathroom, pinching the skin of his nose for twenty minutes at a stretch, not caring who walked in. "Schwarzkopf," Bill Schoepfer used to call him, meaning "blackhead" in pseudo-German. (During the Gulf War, I collected clippings and gave him a fat envelope full: THOUSANDS WELCOME SCHWARZKOPF, SCHWARZKOPF FOR PRESIDENT.) Everyone in the dorm knew you couldn't sit on his bed or touch his pillow, because any failure of cleanliness might, he believed, have dire consequences for his complexion. In the dining hall, he would take an inch-thick stack of paper napkins and patiently blot the grease from every hamburger he ate, pressing one napkin after another against the slimy patties.

Lori reads the invitation, both sides, and asks what this means about blackheads. That's when I remember Suzanne: cleaning his face with Propa pH and a cotton ball, straddling his thighs, breasts swaying inside her T-shirt. "Fun with hygiene," she said.

She was Ugly's cousin, that's how we met her in the first place. She will almost certainly be at the wedding. Has Alan remembered?

He's telling Lori about the time Ugly sneaked a Polaroid of him popping a pimple in the bathroom mirror and taped it to the dorm's front door. Neutral manner, no sign of lightning bolts yet.

Lori checks the spaghetti and calls us to the dinner table, another slab of glass. Alan keeps his hands folded in his lap; I can see the white scar through the tabletop. It may be that he's beyond Suzanne now, safe at last. Or, maybe not.

Beautiful red sauce rests on a bed of spaghetti in the center of each gold-rimmed plate. Steam rises, perfectly. Alan tells another Ugly story, the one about the teddy bear, how he carried it around for a month so he could join the only fraternity on our campus, then got kicked out for puking in the president's Corvette.

"Poor Ugly," I comment when the story's over.

Lori, dismayed, "Does he know you both call him that?"

"Of course not," Alan says.

Her brow is furrowed as she winds her spaghetti around. She's worried about our minor lapses in niceness, oblivous to the lethal past slithering toward her door.

"This is delicious, by the way," I say.

Alan adds, "Really great." Hollow voice, soul elsewhere.

•

Before his tenant can deliver the pool table Alan accepted in lieu of this month's rent (he has yet to evict anyone, though he says he's getting tired of playing social worker), we have to make room in the basement by moving the old refrigerator.

Down the steep, worn wooden steps. Cool breath of mildew, dusty oil tank, nine unframed canvases leaning stacked against a wall. Guests never see this place, only the closest of friends: an honor, really. "Thanks for giving me a hand with this," he says. "You'll have to come shoot pool when the table comes."

"Sounds good to me."

He sets down the dolly, a square of 2x4s with filthy carpeting stapled to two of the four sides, borrowed from the super of his Fort Greene building. The refrigerator is a relic of some long-ago decade, with rounded top and door and raised chrome letters spelling PHILCO. Alan wanted to junk it when they bought the house, but Lori likes having an abundance of food around. He tips the top into my waiting hands and rolls the dolly into the wedge of space. I, on the opposite side, return the refrigerator carefully to the vertical. He's not paying attention, though; the weight of the refrigerator tips the dolly up, my grip fails, a fingernail tears on the chrome letters. Philco lands with a metallic *boom*, squirting the dolly out like a wet bar of soap, and Alan stumbles back into an old tire, which almost knocks over the blackened barbecue.

"You all right?" I ask.

He whisks tire-soot off the back of his T-shirt, nodding. Lori calls down, "What was that?"

"Ow, my toe," I say. Little laugh from above, my reward.

We get it right on the second try. Alan steers the tottering refrigerator to the corner, and on the way knocks down a rusty shovel propped against the wall. So careless: I wonder sometimes how he can run a business.

While we're tipping the refrigerator down off the dolly, he says, "I guess Suzanne'll be at the wedding."

Ah. He waited until we were alone.

"I assume so."

He pulls the dolly away and we stand the refrigerator upright. Bending side by side, we push it the last foot and a half into the corner. Loud scraping, steel against concrete, and the bitter smell of his sweat.

"It's been seven years," he says. "I haven't even passed her on the street."

I fit the greasy, dusty plug into the heavy-duty extension cord, which he plugs into the wall. The motor shudders on.

"You don't have to go to the wedding," I murmur, holding back so much of my voice that it sounds nearly feminine. "You could make up an excuse."

"No, I've been thinking about her a lot lately. I've been wishing I could see her."

Opening the fridge, he plucks two cans of Rolling Rock from their plastic rings and hands me one, forgetting that I hate beer. Sips his while I hold mine. "Are you still getting together with her?" he asks.

Looks right at me. Those green irises—Suzanne called them Mesmer Eyes. I used to imagine the two of them staring into each other and getting lost forever, a coma of love.

I peel a shred from my fingernail. "I haven't seen her for a couple years."

Disappointed, but doesn't ask why I haven't seen her. Lucky for me.

"You know," I say, "I would've thought—I *did* think—you hated her."

"Not at all. It was mostly my fault, I didn't pay attention to the signs. If I'd let her talk about what was bothering her . . . I don't know."

This is news. Alan has rewritten his own history, has reduced their agonies and her last-minute desertion to a simple *If only.* I've never seen anyone do this so blatantly before.

Piled under the steep steps is a warehouse of liquor cartons from their last move. He pulls out one marked *Alan Papers* and removes from it our blue and gold college yearbook.

Leaning it on the laundry sink, he turns the pages. Familiar faces fly by. The page he wants is stuck to the one before it; he peels them apart carefully. Scrap of tape trails from the bottom corner.

Suzanne's face leaps out at us, cat-eyes smiling. I haven't seen this picture in a long time. She's changed since college, her smile has gotten narrower: more irony in it now. What hasn't changed is her hair, black and tangled. Seeing this picture, I hear her voice, the giggling pose of innocence while raining razor blades of candor on us all. "You're such a *sidekick*," she once told me, laughing, the three of us walking to his car in a Roy Rogers parking lot. I stayed away from them for two weeks after that.

So much sex in this face. Unless I'm confusing the face with the memories. Coming back to the room and hearing her screaming climax behind the closed door. That was the closest I'd gotten to sex at the time. Anger at them for parading their wealth before me.

All this in one square inch of black and white.

The breath whistles in and out of Alan's nostrils. Staring. No comment, no disclaimer. Just staring.

Oh boy.

2.

IT'S HARD TO remember clearly what they were like together, everything has changed so much since then. What comes back first is their arms in an X across each others' backs when they walked, in summer T-shirts or winter coats. But what else?

The ends of her hair splashing over her dark shoulders, a black mist. Him burrowing beneath it to kiss the back of her neck. Endless hours of them on his narrow bed with textbooks open while I hid behind my desk to give them privacy. Quiet laughter, *ssh*es, slurpy kisses. Sometimes I peeked at them in the mirror behind me, and saw bare dirty feet, his hand flat on her tan belly, limbs tangled, a loose Indian-print shirt twisting around her as they snuggled and squirmed—until they tiptoed off to shed the last flimsy clothes that separated them. Alan had a key to the equipment room in the basement, and I always imagined them doing it there, standing up.

Their personalities tangled together too. Her playful boldness (she once told a cop his mustache made him look like Stalin) taught Alan to be bolder too, though in a different way: as a clown on the dancefloor, moonwalking and doing old Motown hand-moves with a circle of laughing, clapping people around him. And his romantic sweetness blunted her sharp edges, at least in the beginning.

They were different people then. He wanted to be an accounting professor, and argued with his father on the phone every week, fighting off the pressure to go into business for himself. Suzanne amused herself with clever nonsense all the time, like changing the names they called each other: Harvey and Harvey, Herb and Sherb, Sherpa and Berber. She taught him obscenities in Russian, which I learned too. *Svayo gavno ni vanayit,* Your own shit doesn't stink. *U nivo stayit,* He has a hard-on.

If I were him, I would have hidden from the world and

hoarded my private treasure, but they weren't like that, they used to come for me and invite me along on their outings, never taking no for an answer. We drove to the state park in his mother's hand-me-down Monza, to study outdoors (Suzanne lying on top of him on a flat rock, mouths touching and parting, like kissing Gouramis), and for tours of the tiny towns nearby, where we savored misspelled store signs (e.g., *Ed's Frute*). One night when I was asleep, Suzanne sat on the edge of my bed, her hip against mine, and squeezed my arm to wake me: they wouldn't let me go back to sleep, they insisted I come to Dunkin' Donuts with them. That was the night we kept adding rhyming words to a sentence on a paper napkin, until we had this: "Mark the Narc parked his odd dark ark of bark when the aardvark barked at the mark of the lark"—which seemed to us the most hilarious words ever written.

One drizzly Saturday morning, they bought a foot-tall glass swan at a country flea market, for their future home. Months later, while I was memorizing Italian art terms for a final (*chiaroscuro, quattrocento*), I heard a sneaky giggle and glanced around in the mirror. She was leaning back against him on the bed, her hair still wet from the shower, with the swan between her legs, facing out. The glass tailfeathers rested against her denim fly, and her hand stroked the long neck. It was just playing, silliness, but then Alan slipped his hand into her blouse, and she pressed the swan against herself, and soon they whispered to each other and went away. I locked the door, pulled the windowshade down. Wanted to use the swan somehow, to get just a small piece of what he had, but couldn't figure out a way. The clear blind eyes stared back at me.

It may be that all this adds up to nothing more than the kind of coupling you see on every campus—the sex, the private jokes, the constant touch—but for me Alan and Suzanne defined romance. Kissing in just-cut grass, rolling over each other, green clippings raining from their hair. I wanted that too, exactly what they had. (Still want it. Still haven't found it, not that gorgeous way.)

Along with the bliss, though, came equal and opposite pain. Out of nowhere, always with a giggle, she would slice at him, cut him down from his ecstasy. He said he liked a house we drove by, and she said, leaking contempt through a wide grin, "Dear, isn't it time to mulch the begonias?" By senior year, when the three of us shared an apartment off-campus, her remarks had become more bluntly bludgeoning. ("Just shut up about houses!") He didn't know what to do, would go quiet and pensive, wronged, which made her so furious that she stalked off, a mobile volcano.

They got engaged anyway—went out to Roger K's Steakhouse with his parents and her long-widowed mother, and set a date just after graduation—but in March she ran away, went to work for Pepsi-Cola in Moscow, translating letters and contracts. He disintegrated, and one morning put his hand through our kitchen window. Nearly bled to death: an accident, he claimed.

The swan disappeared. I never found out what happened to it.

•

"He's not so ugly," Lori says.

Alan takes the yearbook without looking away from the road, rests it on the parking brake handle, finds the picture, cracks up. "That bow tie."

Strong sun on the familiar green hills, sweet pangs of memory. Haven't driven this route since we graduated. My nostalgia, while Alan sweats.

"It's not that he was ugly," I explain to Lori. "More like obnoxious. Dumbly confident." Lean forward to look at the picture, the crooked lips and ponytail.

Lori protests, "Obnoxious how?"

I could tell the story of him locking his roommate in the janitor's closet overnight, his idea of a hearty prank, but why bother? He's no more than a subplot today, even if it is his wedding we're going to.

"Look," Alan snorts, inappropriately loud. "Tortoises."

Jane Berger: she wore tight cashmere sweaters, we used to say she had tortoises living on her chest. No comment from Lori, just a questioning smile, *What strange bug has bitten my husband today?*

He flips a page and points merrily, "Maaaah-vin." Bushy eyebrows with dandruff. *Nerdissimo,* we called him.

"Look at all the people who look like animals," I remark, and point: "Horse . . . bird . . . turtle . . . duck . . ."

His eyes squint down to laughing slits, tears from the crinkled corners. Going 15 miles an hour over the limit.

Pages turn, faces pass. Sonia Nesselroth, who smelled. (What if, at the end of your life, the only thing people remember about you is B. O.?) Walter Nesbit, who later ran for supervisor of his small town and lost to a furniture salesman.

We're getting perilously close to Suzanne's page. Close the book, Alan.

Last-minute swerve to avoid a dead raccoon. Onto the gravelly shoulder, skidding, until he steers out of it.

"Ahem," I say, and take the yearbook into the back seat.

"Maybe you should pull over and stretch," Lori suggests, and he snaps at her, "I'm not tired."

Nothing I can do to help. So, flip through the yearbook in search of beautiful faces. Trampy but smart Holly Carvalho, maternal Pia Noone, waiflike Tanya Stotz. I had four years to pursue them, and never dared. Nor am I sure I would dare now.

The road rises between the blasted-out halves of a hill. Vertical dynamite channels intersect tan and copper strata, the past preserved in rock. A route back through time.

Alan points to the Red Barn Diner in its gleaming railroad car; I explain to Lori, "The barn burned down in the Fifties." Landmarks keep whizzing by. The defunct chemical factory, reincarnated now as a shopping center with striped awnings. The Crystal Teacup, front window still crowded with the wallet-size yearbook photos of every waitress who ever worked there. The massive brown and white bull on the roof of Roger K's Steakhouse, paint flaking from the chest, *It's Kool Inside* decal still on the door. The Tiny Town That Time Forgot, we used to say.

Off Main Street and over the train tracks: a detour. Lori gazes out amiably as we turn into the dead-end of Hudson Street. Down the hill, toward the weedy railroad embankment.

Alan parks alongside the peeling gray box. Rests his hands in his lap, looks at the house, doesn't explain to his wife—so I do. "This is where we lived, the last year and a half of school."

"Did it look like this then?"

"Worse. The doors were green."

Three sagging stories, each with a porch across the front. Around the side, can't see it from here, is the kitchen window. Because of the hill, there was grass at the height of the windowsill. We used to toss peanuts out to a squirrel we called Rocky. Our upstairs neighbor, Norbert—a perpetually smiling carpenter from an even smaller town than Gold River, we called him the Jigsaw Killer—was walking back toward the garage when he saw Alan's arm hanging out the window, bleeding on the grass. He was the one who called the ambulance; I was at school. When I got home, he told me what he had seen: Alan slumped over on the kitchen table, his head on the windowsill surrounded by jagged glass. Same table, same window where we fed Rocky. (And now, because of nerve damage, Alan has no sensation on the back of that hand. A permanent reminder.)

"You must have a lot of memories here," Lori says.

Yellow and orange marigolds in Nike shoeboxes on the windowsill. Maybe Alan's thinking not about the broken window, but about the idyllic afternoons we spent studying on this porch, sharing plastic pitchers of instant iced tea. The time we read tedious sentences aloud from our textbooks, vying for the most stupefying.

A dirty-faced boy in a diaper comes toddling out the open door with a red toy hammer. Alan puts the Mazda back in gear, does a broken U, and takes us back up the hill without a word.

Diagramming a pattern on the palm of his hand, Alan tells me to stay in close. Four against four; the only ones I know are Alan, Ugly and Joe, Ugly's shy, depressive college roommate. Soup-thick heat, smell of mowed grass, and two fears: that I will snap what's left of the reconstructed ligament in my knee, and worse, that Alan will shoot me one of his bullets and I'll drop it, just like long ago. We line up—there's the gold onion dome of the Slavic church, down in the lush valley—and Ugly flips the ball to Alan, starts counting. Guy covering me sticks like a Band-Aid as I cut left. The pattern's done, nothing left now but to zig and zag, Ugly's up to seven Mississippi and Alan still can't find a receiver. I get clear for a moment, he sees me but keeps searching. Finally, drills one to the musclebound little guy in the tank-top, who gains a few extra yards before getting tagged. "Baby!" Alan shouts, charged up, unrecognizable from ten minutes ago, when we sat in the car in the near-empty lot and he kept flicking the little baseball at the end of his keychain, keeping it swinging from the ignition. He wanted to talk about Suzanne, I assumed, but couldn't begin, not even when I asked how he was doing—and then Ugly yelled, "Schwarzkopf!" and out we went.

New line of scrimmage, same pattern for me but this time I get the pass, boom in the chest, my glasses fall off but my hands surround the ball. Forget the glasses and run. "He's blind," someone yells, "stop him before he hurts himself!" Pushed out of bounds, pebbly brown ball clutched in my hands, *Made in Korea, Inflate 13 Lbs.* Alan hands me my glasses and slaps my hand: redemption. Next he scores by running around Ugly, and we're all streaming sweat, gnats hanging over us, but we've come home, to the magic triangle between the Admin, Physical Science and library towers, brick and glass and faded green aluminum, the nondescript place where we were happy and together and ruled the world.

Ugly's turn to quarterback. Corporate hair now, no more

pony-tail, but the same puffed-out chest, a braggart bird. Joe bobbles a pass, drops it, and Ugly moans, "Ayayayayay," no mercy even for his best friend and best man. I'm close to passing out from the heat and humidity—whose idea was this anyway, and how do the Miami Dolphins do it? Next, Ugly sends everyone out long and tries to run around Alan, get his revenge, but Alan pursues ferociously, dives to make the tag, knocks Ugly off his feet. Stumble and sprawl, Ugly's chin skidding through a clump of buttercups into the concrete curb. He gets up to show he's okay, still in possession of the ball, but his left leg folds under him.

One of his friends is a dermatologist now, and he examines the ankle while Joe dabs the bleeding chin with his own balled-up T-shirt. The rest of us stand around uselessly, except for Alan, who kneels next to the victim, sickly gray with remorse. Ugly shoves him over on the grass, "Nice work, shmuck"—but it's a joke, his first chance ever to taunt Alan about a stupid mistake. The dermatologist and best man help him up, he limps between them. "Biggest day of my life and he breaks my leg."

The rest of us crack up—except Alan, who mumbles to me, "I don't know how I'm going to get through this."

•

Across the hot-as-hell parking lot, Alan dapper in a glen plaid summer suit, Lori's dress swinging with her stride, me in my $99 special (can everyone tell?) and an old tie of my father's with little red medallions. CONGRATULATIONS GERALD & DEBORAH says the marquee below the Holiday Inn sign. Couples converge on the glass doors, many familiar faces. We were a messy-haired, wrinkly-shirted bunch, but everyone looks so sharp today.

"You're crushing my hand," Lori tells Alan.

"He's just afraid Ugly'll come down the aisle in a wheelchair."

Into the cool lobby. There's the groom, posing for a photo by the indoor waterfall. Gray tux, gray patent leather shoes, no crutches. Prettier bride than I expected, scolding her mother.

Suzanne here yet? Not that I can see.

Boisterous greetings, hearty handshakes, Alan introducing Lori around. Acting normal, even enthusiastic. Quite a feat.

Folding chairs have been set up with an aisle down the center. Tinkling on the piano cues us to sit. Alan between us, beefy young woman with chin-stubble to my right. Two of the catering crew carry trellises with plastic ivy up the center aisle and set up an instant arbor behind the huppah.

Alan, Lori's hand in his lap, glances around the room, stiff-jawed.

The rabbi swaddles the wineglass in its napkin. Ugly limps up to the huppah, face pale, chest hollow, no more braggart bird. Still no Suzanne. Could be she decided not to come, to avoid the scene that has made Alan anxious—no, terrified—for weeks.

A delay, whispers. The flower girl has spilled orange soda on her dress. Now something classical on the electric piano, and here come the bridesmaids in matching violet gowns, on the arms of ushers. The bride, supported by a parent on each arm, makes her way anemically through a storm of flashes, like a celebrity widow. Can't help wondering how Ugly snared this beauty. Nasty theories about his income and his genitals.

The ceremony is mostly in Hebrew. A few familiar phrases, *elohaynu melech haw-olom,* still don't know what it means. The goateed rabbi lectures on ring-symbolism, then bride and groom repeat some Hebrew after him. A "New York" sneaks in amid the ancient syllables, eliciting chuckles.

Door opens behind us, letting in the sound of vacuuming in the lobby, then closes again. Glancing back, I see Suzanne—trying to slip in unseen, failing, and smiling with irony at the failure. She has on a long, flowing dress, snug on top but made modest by an embroidered vest, maybe

Guatemalan. Despite the coverup, she has instantly become the most desirable woman in this room.

There is murmuring, and in it, her name. Alan doesn't turn around.

Tanner than I've ever seen her, she could pass for an Arab. Wider, leaning toward overweight, but it doesn't matter. She sees me and gives a little lift of the eyebrows, knowing I understand. I nod back. It's like being friends with Marilyn Monroe.

She takes a seat in the back. The rabbi enumerates the many interpretations of the smashing of the glass, then Ugly does it. Mazel tovs, hugging at the huppah, exit bride and groom and attendants. Ugly proud as he goes by, limping but exultant, afraid no more.

I'd forgotten this was a wedding.

•

Cocktail hour, drinks all around. Band with toupeed trumpeter plays tame rock, hardworking caterers roll in a dozen plywood tabletops, the chapel turns into a dinner hall with a dance floor. Alan tells Ugly's friend Joe how he became a landlord: was an accountant, hated it, went with his cousin to look at a building, the cousin thought there were too many vacancies, but Alan got excited and borrowed money from family, took possession, *then* discovered the problems.

Suzanne, chatting nearby with relatives, never glances this way. I've heard Alan's story before and this drink, my third, is making me fidgety. Check out the women: anyone appealing? Yes, but all taken.

A shrunken grandfather eats a pat of butter, his elderly daughter groans, "Pop, stop," and he says, "What? It is banana." As I'm leaning to share this with Lori, Suzanne makes her move. Friendly smile as she approaches, but she's standing oddly straight, as if a hidden puppeteer had pulled a string at the top of her head taut.

Too late to flee.

Alan must have had an eye on her all along, because he turns now, giving her his back as he goes on with his story—how the building turned out to be rent-regulated, with a cracked boiler and lots of crumbling mortar outside.

Suzanne changes course and heads out of the room.

Lori to me, quiet so as not to interfere with Alan's anecdote, "I was just thinking about your toast at our wedding. Can you still recite it?"

I can, but don't want to right now. Here comes my rescuer, a waiter asking us to please find our tables.

My placecard has a different number than theirs, which can only mean one thing. I put my hand on Alan's shoulder, *Good luck,* then it's off to face my own smaller ordeal.

The singles table.

Guy with three rows of transplanted hair-plugs above his forehead. Two giggling dorks whose names I never knew, Ugly's friends. Frail pallid woman with thick, pink-tinted glasses hunched over her glass of water. The stubble-chinned woman writing on the back of a postcard, using time efficiently, expecting nothing from tonight.

I hate this. Don't want to know them, have no interest in their hidden qualities, just want to spend the evening with my friends.

"Burt?"

What, who . . . Bleached golden bangs, dark eyeshadow, a snug lavender minidress. Not the kind of person who knows my name, usually.

"It's Holly," she says.

"Holly Carvalho!" My yearbook fantasy, *trampy but smart.* "What are you doing here?" (She remembered my name—Holly of the parted lips, gapped bangs echoing gapped front teeth, from a small town upstate. Spoke to her maybe once in four years of college.)

"I lived on Debbie's floor," she says, that cute rural accent, and sits next to me. "What about you?"

"I lived in Gerry's suite for a year."

Thick, candy-like perfume fogs me in. We sit. "What a relief to know somebody," Holly says.

"Ditto, exclamation point."

She laughs, though it wasn't really that witty, which may mean she's interested. There's too much mascara crusted on her lashes, but I don't care. "So where do you live now and what do you do and all that kind of stuff?"

Another laugh—Mr. Lucky! "I just moved to New York City—"

A touch on my shoulder, from behind.

Suzanne.

"Mind if I hide here with you?"

Bends to kiss me, and my shoulder presses into her belly. Familiar baby-powder scent cuts through Holly's sugar. Pain in her wide smile, a friend in need.

Damn.

The dorks shift over, freeing up the seat to my left. I introduce Holly and Suzanne, who know each other by sight, they say. Others at the table watch us. *This guy must have hidden qualities.*

There is a red rose etched onto each of the white porcelain beads in Suzanne's necklace. Her earrings are wooden parrots, yellow, red and orange. I'd forgotten this: along with the flesh come these intriguing details. You just want to keep looking at her.

"I missed my bus at the Port Authority. You look handsome in your suit."

Holly eases back into her chair. We were both leaning forward, didn't notice until now.

"You look great too." Holly drinking her drink, watching the musicians drink theirs. "Holly just told me she lives in New York now."

"Oh!"

Teasing me for that worse-than-lame attempt at conversation. Even in distress, she keeps a sharp edge.

A waiter makes his way around the table, offering choices for dinner. As we wait for him, I count the men who are staring at Suzanne: bartender, three uncles, pianoplayer, even the two dorks. It's the combination of her flesh and her smile: you see luscious bodies and you see beguil-

ing smiles, but not often on the same person. Even the shrunken old butter-eating zayde keeps a watery red eye on her as he conducts his imaginary orchestra with a spoon.
Even Alan. A steady, grim gaze.
"Herbed chicken breast or prime rib? Both are served with mixed green salad and confetti orzo pasta." (Wo, Manhattan comes to Gold River. What's orzo?)
Chicken for all but Suzanne. "I thought you couldn't digest beef," I say.
"No, that was before the surgery. All I have to do now is avoid fats and oils. That's how I got so chunky."
"Not quite."
"Oh Burt, you charmer."
But I've left Holly alone for too long.
"Holly, I don't even know what you do."
"I'm an actuary at New York Life."
Best not to chuckle at the incongruity. "So, you figure out how long New Yorkers will probably live?"
"Something like that."
"No, really. What do you do all day?"
"I price products, with mortality tables. How much an annuity should cost if it's supposed to pay x dollars for the rest of your life."
"Ah."
Suzanne sipping her water, hiding a smile. She gets it now, that I'm in pursuit. Let her smirk.
Fuzzy from the three drinks and two perfumes, I can't seem to get my treasure-chest of repartee unlocked. "Where in the city do you live?"
Quiet and far away, "85th and 1st."
This isn't working. Give up. Especially now that my hand, en route to a roll and butter, has knocked over my club soda. Hurry, fumbling, blot the tablecloth with linen napkin.
"Better pour some red wine on that," Suzanne says.
The dorks guffaw.
At last, dinner. Cut the chicken carefully into small pieces, don't be seen ramming hunks of meat down my gul-

let. And now Suzanne murmurs in my ear, so good to feel her warm breath there, "I don't know what I would have done if you weren't here."

Remember now that I like her—though of course I would never dare to desire her again, any more than I would volunteer to ride a lightning bolt.

Hair transplant and pink glasses commiserate during the meal about the forthcoming bar exam and their prep courses. The rest of us strive for silent dignity as the loud chatter of other tables engulfs us.

Suddenly Suzanne sits straight. Alan's coming this way. Alone.

It's like when I exited the Grand Central Parkway, hit an oil slick, and surfed into the guardrail: no sound, no heartbeat, nothing in the world but slowed-down time and the impending collision.

Suzanne wipes her hands on her napkin, under the tablecloth. Ten feet from the table, however, Alan swerves away and heads for the door to the lobby, same escape route Suzanne used.

"I get the feeling I'm poison," she says.

"No, it's not that."

"I think maybe I should leave."

"No, he *wants* to talk to you. He's just built this up so much in his mind."

"It looks simpler than that to me. It looks like he can't stand the sight of me."

"Don't go anywhere, I'll be right back."

Stand carefully—bad idea to drink so much, which way is vertical?—cross the dance floor and exit.

In the men's room, Alan coaxing some curls into the bays in his hairline. Sees me in the mirror and stops. Tired eyes and sweat.

"She isn't going out with anyone?"

"She didn't say."

Washes his hands slowly, thoroughly. Leaving a sink between us, I run cold water on my wrists to push away the haze.

"She's put on weight."

"It's since her surgery. Actually, it's a sign of health."

Stare like a steel rod. "What surgery?"

Right, he had no way of knowing. "You remember her stomach problems. They had to remove part of her ileum. She's fine now, she just has to watch her diet."

Angrily, "Why didn't—"

Censors himself, too late. Why didn't I tell him? Because I wasn't allowed to speak her name for seven years, that's why.

Sunken face. Grief for the inch or so of intestine they took out of her. Or for their separation—that she could go under the knife without him knowing.

"She's really okay."

Two gray-haired men in sports jackets come in to piss, grumbling. "Six hours in the car when they both live in New York. It makes no sense."

Quietly, to Alan, "Just come talk to her. Get it over with. She thinks you despise her."

A wince. Good.

Best man Joe is finishing what must have been a very short toast. Bubbles rise in a hundred raised champagne glasses while he gropes for eloquence. "So, let's all wish them both the best of the best. They deserve it. They deserve everything."

"He's worse at this than I was," say I to Alan, but Alan is gone, striding over to the band, whispering to the trumpet-player, who says through his mike, "Don't sit down, ladies and gentlemen, we have another toast."

Back to the singles table, where Suzanne leans her head on my shoulder. I know it's about him, not me, but there's a tingling nevertheless.

Ten guys cheer when Alan takes the mike. "We talked about Gerry in the car on the way up. Trying to come up with the one story that captured what he was like." A benign way to put it. "But instead we just kept remembering different stories. And that's what we realized about him. He's a dynamo, the kind of guy who's always bringing life and laughter to his friends."

What a smooth liar. Cast a glance at Lori, the only other one who knows he made this up. She's staring four inches to my right, at Suzanne. Engrossed, disturbed.

And what is Suzanne doing? Watching Alan in fondness and sorrow.

"Everyone here who lived in our dorm knows what I mean. Like the night he got us to bury the lecture hall doors in snow, and they had to cancel classes the next day. Or when he locked Joe in the broom closet overnight. We had an accounting class together, and one time he started tossing pistachio nuts at me. Whenever the professor turned to write on the board, he threw a nut, and I had to catch it so the professor wouldn't hear it land."

Laughter all around. He's so good at this, should have been a toastmaster. Allows himself only a hair's-breadth glance at Suzanne.

"Gerry, I just want to say, to you and Debbie, that it's great to see you together. Everyone here loves you, and we wish you all the happiness two people can share."

War-whoops and whistles. Gerry so moved, he stumps across the room like Walter Brennan to give Alan a bearhug. Dork to dork, "I thought he'd do something funnier." Hair guy to pink glasses, "That was a good toast."

"Burt," Suzanne says, "can we go outside?"

She looks queasy, weak. And Holly? Wiping lipstick from her champagne glass, checking her watch, no longer recognizing my existence. Shit but oh well.

Out through the lobby, past the waterfall, to the parking lot. Muggy out, bugs swarming around the amber lights in the bushes under the Holiday Inn sign. Suzanne takes from her purse a slim silver case engraved with Art Nouveau arabesques, pops it open, and slips one of four joints from under the elastic ribbon. "This isn't a good night," she says. Brass lighter in the shape of a rifle cartridge provides a flame; she starts the joint and passes it to me. Okay, sure, what the hell.

"There's no place I could possibly fit in his life." She takes back the joint. Long inhale, the narrow tip glows.

"I didn't know you wanted a place in his life."

Inside, the band starts "Ain't Too Proud to Beg," but not much of it penetrates the glass and the noise of cicadas. Instead of answering me, she asks, "Do you think married people pity us?"

"No, I think they envy our supposed sexual adventures."

Tinkly laugh. "I miss you."

I miss her too, now that I see her again, but can't say so without sounding like a stooge. Awkward gap where the *Me too* would have gone.

"Are you comfortable being a bachelor?" she asks.

"The opposite. It's humiliating, having no one, or so many brief someones. Why do you ask?"

She nods at the newlyweds. Gerry dancing foolishly, arms flailing, in bliss. "You can't help being happy for them—but you *know* they're going to torture each other for the rest of their lives. Still, maybe that's better than loneliness."

Careful, Burt. She does this: lures you close and then bites your head off.

"I never thought of you as lonely."

"No one I've gone out with since college has loved me the way Alan did. And vice versa. It took me years to realize what a mistake I made."

She looks up at the campus, at the three dark towers on the hill. A red light blinks on top of the library, where we read *Crime and Punishment* side by side, me in English, her in Russian.

"I dreaded coming here. Every little shrub reminds me of some moment with him." Nods at the Dunkin' Donuts down the road. "Remember when we wrote that long, silly sentence on the napkin?"

"Yep."

"I kept remembering that when I was sick in Moscow. It seemed like paradise."

"I'm surprised. Considering."

She ignores that and holds the joint up, *Want it?* No, uh-uh. Two shakes of the head, because the first was so feeble she might have missed it.

Wistfully, "How is he doing these days?"

"He's good. Okay."

"His wife looks nice."

"She is. She's a sweet person."

Fly buzzing around my head. Shake it off.

"When I think about what I did to him, I want to cut my throat."

As far as I know, she never heard about the hand through the window. In other words, she doesn't know the full extent of her crime. Impulse to tell her, but have mercy, she's suffering enough.

Her crooked smile could mean many things. Or else just one thing: here comes Alan, with Lori. She hands me the joint, which I hide behind my leg, as if they were our parents.

Alan squeezes my arm just above the elbow, meant as an emblem of friendship but more like a cop nabbing a perp. He delivers a controlled Hi, to be shared by Suzanne and me. Then, "Suzanne, this is my wife, Lori."

He left something out, some empty pleasantry like *Long time no see*, what one would say if one's guts weren't intricately knotted.

The women shake hands. "It's good to finally meet you," says freckled, slender Lori. Suzanne, twice her size, replies with equal warmth, "It is."

We're all so nimble and polite.

Alan—brooding face over loud suit—asks his lost love, "What are you up to these days?"

"I work at a place that helps Russian immigrants get settled."

"What do you do there?" Lori asks.

"Reassure them, mostly. Calm them down. My supervisor wants me to get them into vocational programs so they don't go on welfare, but I spend most of my time just letting them talk. It takes a while for them to adjust. They do, though, more or less. I couldn't deal with counseling people who never got better."

"She has an MSW," I throw in, so that Alan at least knows the bare outlines.

"What about you?" she asks him. "Is your business going well?"

As he explains himself (reserved, defending against possible scorn) I notice the rectilinear pattern of his glen plaid suit, as contrasted with the swirling gold sequins on her vest. How far they have evolved, in such different directions. Wonder if they're thinking the same thing.

"It's an education," he says. "When I started, I didn't know anything, but I've learned a lot."

"What kinds of things?"

"Well. My first building had a shot boiler, and rent-regulated tenants. I never should have bought it."

"Sounds complicated."

"What's really complicated is dealing with the City."

"The bureaucracy?"

"That and the pure bullshit. They just raised water rates, and called it a conservation measure, but apartments aren't individually metered, so who's going to use less water? The City is worse than a hundred crazy tenants."

Showing more of himself than I expected. *This is what I've become, I refuse to pretend for you.*

"Suzanne, tell them about that chemical engineer you helped, the one who named his new glue after you."

Lori says, "Really? That's so nice."

"My one claim to fame. Susanka Super-Sticky."

Despite the heat, Alan puts both hands in his pants pockets. Frowning down at his shoes, jingling his change. Seven years of waiting, and this is all he gets—nothing, a waste, useless pain.

The music inside has turned Jewish, they're playing "Sholom Aleichem." A circle is forming.

"Burt, let's go dance," says Lori.

Startled, nervous laugh from me, because her motive is

so obvious. But all right, if she wants to let them have their reunion in private, it's her marriage, not mine.

From the sloppy, lively hora circle, holding Lori's cool hand and an angelic little girl's, I look for Alan and Suzanne each time we come around opposite the broad window. They keep their backs to us, like gangsters hiding from lipreaders. Alan gesturing, Suzanne nodding.

The songs flow into each other, "Tzena, Tzena," "Siman Tov Umazel Tov," "L'Chaim." Across from us, Holly loses her balance and a grinning old lech supports her by the elbow. Then Alan and Suzanne are gone.

He has a motel room just across the parking lot. Yikes. (He always gets what he wants, damn him—because he wants it more than I dare to want anything.)

Lori, oblivious, keeps turning her shoulders to the side, one of the few who really know how to do this dance. Serene smile, miles above jealousy. If the foundation of her life cracks apart, there will be nothing to hold her up. Will she become embittered and solitary, or just snap, go passively insane and forget to wipe the crumbs from her mouth?

But I'm wrong, I'm all wrong, because here comes Alan, breaking through the circle and grabbing Gerry by the hand, dragging him into the center. Now they're back to back, kazatskying like vodka-flushed Cossacks, the guys from our freshman floor shouting, "Go! Go! Go!"—and for a moment I'm back in the lounge of Otsego Hall, watching drunken Alan perform Michael Jackson routines on a tabletop, shining with sweat, eyes half-closed, a dancing demon.

Gerry drops to the floor, panting and laughing. The band finishes with a klezmerish chord, our hands unclasp and loudly clap, and Alan tries to swing Gerry around in a circle of two. Gerry says, "He's crazy!" and pulls away to find his bride.

The trumpet plays the five-note hook of "You Really Got Me." Alan dazed, surrounded by people he doesn't recognize. "He hasn't drunk this much in a long time," Lori says, and goes to him. He grabs her and dances her around in a frenetic Lindy, ignoring the music.

Holly alone as the couples sort out around her. I've got little to lose. Cross the floor, "Would you like to?"

A nod, looking off at nothing in particular, and then we're dancing. My inner thighs ache from football, but the hard part is over. Take Holly's hands, pull her closer.

Two more fast songs, then the tempo slows by half, "Every Breath You Take." Holly puts her arms on my shoulders, and now I can hold her waist, her hot back. Squeeze her against me, and she accepts, even tips her head against the side of mine. My sweat would embarrass me except that she's sweating just as much, I can smell it on her scalp through the perfume.

Alan half asleep, his forehead leaning against Lori's, home safe. Guests handing Gerry envelopes, which he holds up to the light as a joke and then stashes in a bulging jacket pocket. Suzanne talking to Gerry's parents, her aunt and uncle; smile not quite wide enough to cover the pain.

"Oh can't you see," Holly whisper-sings, guiding me to the next words of the song, *you belong to me.* My hand creeps into her hair (never touched bleached hair before, it's not as coarse as I expected) and then she puts her fingers in my hair too. Squeeze closer, thighs between thighs. A dream come true, a beauty who desires me. In my brain, ten thousand light-bulbs spell the words, AT LAST.

But Suzanne: by herself now, leaning back against the tiny flowers of the wallpaper, twirling a red carnation in her fingers. Watching Alan and Lori sway together, four eyes closed. Granting them their life, while she bravely endures the sorrow she made for herself.

3.

"Jim . . . likes the . . . often—office at . . . nine—dammit—night. It is . . . quiet."

"Good."

Don't want to be here, tutoring Ernie Edwards for the fourth week in a row because his teacher said he disrupted the group and the director doesn't know what else to do with him. Crowded together in my cubicle, under the flickering fluorescent—at least give me a window, let me see the sun. Or else let me undress Holly again, her hips in my hands, such soft skin, flat on her belly, cursing with pleasure, can scarcely believe it happened. Call her tonight, try for a repeat.

"He . . . didn't—didn't?"

"Sound it out."

"Don't—doesn't. Doesn't? . . . have . . . to . . . take—talk." Puts his broad fingernail on the book to hold his place. "He like the job 'cause he can't talk to no one? What kind of story is that?"

Ernie goes through teachers like a drill through soft wood, not only because of slow progress (he tested recently at Level 3.5 for letter/sound recognition and Level 2 for comprehension, an advance of half a grade after two years) but because he blurts out his unpopular opinions and then curls up like an armadillo when contradicted. Actually, the inability to read is the least of his problems. He goes to alcoholism counseling and some kind of vocational training, and got hit by a bus this past spring, which put him in the hospital for six weeks. He has two illegitimate children, but only one index finger. The differences between us would matter less if he ever looked me in the eye or shook my hand. Instead, he slips away mumbling after every session, and I can't tell if it's a black/white thing, or a psychiatric problem, or that he just can't stand me.

"Would *you* want a job with no one to talk to?"

"Sometimes I think I wouldn't mind."

Big mistake: he understood perfectly. Now he has one more reason to dislike me, and also to feel like shit.

Goes back to reading, somber and mechanical. "Jim... opens—"

"No, that's a long word."

Go back to this morning's dream. Something about Laura Dern and a swimming pool, pornographic but sweet. I'm delivering a package, she's annoyed, mocks me. When I kiss her, though, she looks deep into my eyes, was only waiting for someone to love her so she could be human again. Where did it go after that? Someplace green, a meadow or golf course. Bring it back, or lose it forever.

"Opportunity? Op—er..."

This job steals my dreams.

"Read past it, see if you can figure it out."

"Jim . . . mm . . . a . . . vanish—"

"Not vanish."

Twists his neck inside the tight plaid collar, made tighter by the knitted tie. "I don't know this word. Never saw it. What kind of word got two U's?"

"Look at the picture, it'll remind you."

Photo-illustration of a joyless white guy in his twenties, operating an industrial vacuum cleaner. The wonderful world of work.

"What he got? Look like a trash barrel."

"It's a vacuum cleaner. Remember?"

He slaps my desk, mad at himself. Next to where he slapped, a grant application lies in wait, file thick as a finger, deadline closing in, though the thought of starting makes me grateful for any delay. I've come a long way since the days when this job made me proud every morning: such a noble vocation, literacy above a Pentecostal church on 125th Street. All I do lately, though, except for tutoring Ernie, is write grant proposals, the same sales pitch over and over. *We believe every human being has the right to ownership of the written word.* (Boss' language, not mine.) Much of what I write is simple truth, but even so, when you say it over and over, it feels like a lie. And there *is* a lie of omission built into every fundraising and promotional piece we send out: no one goes from pre-literate to GED here, or anywhere I know of. The students learn slowly, they reach plateaus and get stuck, they quit. But my job is to describe the successes. *Ethel B. couldn't read a subway map, now she can travel anywhere in the city in her job as a home health aide. She says, "Literacy Action gave me the most beautiful gift in the world. The freedom to understand."* I must have typed these words five hundred times; sometimes they put me in a trance halfway through. Or is the word *stupor?*

"Try the sentence again."

Weary sigh. "Jim . . . op-er-ates—"

"Yes! Good!"

"A   vac-son   cleaning."

"That's 'vacuum cleaner.'"

He shifts in his chair. "Why they got you in such a small office?"

"Because I'm a small guy. Back to work."

He reads two sentences, distracting me from memories of Holly, then pauses.

"Butt."

He's calling me.

"How long till I take my GED?"

Bloodshot eyes.

"You have to go one step at a time."

"Next year?"

Let me preserve a grain of honesty amid all the encouragement. "No. It'll take longer than that."

"They said the same thing in my alcoholic group. Guess I'm just stupid."

"No, everyone has some goal that feels far away. That doesn't make you stupid."

Skeptically, challenging, "You got one too?"

"Sure. I guess it would be, to accomplish something worth doing in the world."

Some spit, sprayed with his laugh, hits the back of my

hand. "You better look out for yourself. Let the world do what the world gonna do."

Legitimate opinion, yet it makes me want to knock his chair over. "Let's read some more. We still have five minutes."

"Man, you always cracking the whip."

He's right, I should give him a break, work on something easier, maybe silent reading for comprehension, but I don't have the energy to change course. He returns grudgingly to the place his finger kept. "He . . . go—goes . . . into . . . each . . . off—offer—opening—office and . . . cleans . . . the . . . car—carpet?"

Nod. Shift my feet; one hits his shoe. "Sorry." No room to move here.

"Some . . . times . . . doing—"

"During. Say 'durrrrr.' "

"Durrrr."

"Durrrring."

"Durrrrrrrrring."

"Good."

"—doing . . . the . . . night"

No. No, Ernie. This is not good. This is not my goal. I won't sit here with you until I die.

"he . . . for—forty—What that word?"

"Forgets."

Get me out of here, let me see the sky again. Let me leave, and find something else to do with my life.

"forgets . . . his . . . at . . . work . . . and . . . im—impossible?"

"Imagines."

"imagines . . . his . . . some . . . place . . . far . . . away."

Five o'clock. Time to go.

•

Jean-Claude, our Haitian computer coordinator, slides into second and raises a cloud of dust that drifts, golden in the late-day sunlight, into our eyes. The shortstop takes a mock-genteel step back from the cloud, *We don't slide in softball.* Thirty blocks south, beyond trees and pond and castle, the slanting light falls on the towers of midtown, turning their western faces molten. The park and city are so beautiful, it's as if I just arrived from some wretched foreign shore and am seeing happiness for the first time.

We're playing Friendship Home, a residence for the mentally ill, one of the few teams in the non-profit league that let clients play. The pitcher, in a Mets cap, has been talking himself through the game since the first inning. "It's all up to me, gotta hold 'em, the chips are down." Alan leaning back against the chain-link backstop, fidgeting with the knotted leather thong at the tip of his mitt's pinky. (There is no softball league for entrepreneurs, so he plays with us, a ringer.) I want to tell him about my resolution to leave Literacy Action, but don't want my co-workers in the dugout to hear.

Patty at bat, my main friend at work, I'd ask her out if she weren't gay. "Heyyyyyy, battabattabatta," calls some fool. Outfielders have moved in to the scrubby edge where dirt meets grass, standard procedure with female batters, but they're in for a surprise. First pitch, *pow*, into right field and no one with a glove anywhere near it.

"I decided to change careers," I venture under my breath as Patty rounds the bases to screams of appreciation.

"I can't stop thinking about Suzanne," Alan says.

A little cough is all I can get out. Wish I could vanish, cut him off right there, and so protect us both from havoc.

"I thought I would just get over it, but I can't. I keep wanting to call her."

"Yowza."

"I'm not sure I can stop myself." Striving to keep his voice calm, but can't suppress the tremble. "I haven't felt this way in so long. I keep remembering what it used to be like. I don't know what to do—it's like I'm coming out of my skin."

Foul ball hits the equipment bag next to my foot, releasing a puff of field dust. Toss it back to the pitcher. I have a job to do: talk Alan away from the edge of the cliff. "What about everything you went through?"

"I know, that's what I keep telling myself. But then I think, we were only twenty, she was right to back off, that's too young to get married. When I talked to her at the wedding, I had the feeling she missed me."

My co-workers trotting out to the field, Friendship Home coming in. Three outs already?

"I guess we'll continue this next inning," I say.

In left field there are vast meadows of time, for reflection or avoidance of reflection. Look, there's the Fuji blimp over the G. M. Building. (Ground-hugging sizzler to Alan at short, bad hop off a pebble but he rises and scoops it up by the hip, graceful even in obsession.) *I'd* like him to have his old bliss back too, would even donate a portion of my future happiness to help, but if he got involved with Suzanne, history would repeat itself, and then Lori would find out, and he'd end up with no one. (Long ball, way past me, I'm fast but not fast enough, out here alone, chasing it onto the paved path and beyond, past mellow picknickers alarmed by my sprinting, finally comes to rest in a tuft of weeds, turn to throw and there's the batter crossing home. Stupid game, how is it that one instant I can be weighing my best friend's fate, and the next I drop it to chase a dirty ball?)

Three outs, Alan joins me near third base. Both of us looking at our sneakers instead of at each other. Cinnamon infield dirt on four white socks.

"You were saying?"

"I feel like I've been in suspended animation all this time. I want to call her."

"Don't you think you may be idealizing the past?"

"At the wedding" (guess he's not going to respond to my gentle understatement) "when we were alone outside, she kept asking about my business. I think she really wanted to talk about *us*, but wouldn't let herself. What do you think? If I were available, would she try again?"

He's staring at me like sun through a magnifying glass.

"I have no way of guessing."

"When I remember what it used to be like, nothing else seems worth having. I've been thinking about going to her apartment, just to watch her go in. Pretty insane, right?"

It's not pleasant to step in front of a moving train.

"Let me tell you what I think. You want this more than anything, I understand that."

Interruption: our batters have gone down, one two three, time for us to take the field again. Ridiculous game.

Alan intercepts Rohan, our fiscal director and team manager. "I have to leave early, I have an appointment."

"I've got to go too, Rohan. Sorry we forgot to tell you."

Annoyed, but it's okay, they still have nine if they put Jean-Claude's wife in right field.

Freed, we head toward the West Side. Cute kids toss pebbles in the pond, scaring the ducks. Alan waits stoically for my sermon. The trick is to find words he's not expecting, words he can't dismiss. "I think there are situations where—it's like being a drug addict. The thing you crave most is the thing that will destroy you. If you went back to her, you would lose everything you have, and then you would lose her too."

Heart pounding. I've never spoken to him this way, contradicting his deepest wishes. His glove, held by the backstrap, flops against his leg with each step. His quiet answer: "I've told myself the same thing. But it doesn't make it any easier."

I put my hand on his shoulder. Through his T-shirt comes a terrible heat.

His mouth has turned down, a familiar sour expression. Take the hand away, it's not wanted.

•

Clean from the shower, time to call Holly. The prospect of inviting her here, though, reveals my apartment in a stark light. Mandela T-shirt covering stained back cushion of the easy chair my mother bought at Gimbel's on my third birthday, my earliest memory. Yellowed political cartoons taped to the kitchen wall, reddish circles where simmering sauces spattered them. Books everywhere. She won't get the lifestyle, will size me up as a loser.

Resolved: I'll clean house, shop for furniture after work tomorrow, throw out as much as I can bear to.

Her number on a sheet of Holiday Inn notepaper. Memory of her skin, how soft it was. Ignore the fear, concentrate on the desire. Dial. Go ahead. No more delaying.

Now.

Now.

"Holly? It's Burt."

"Hi, Burt."

Two tired, descending notes that tell me her answer: *I've been waiting for this call, you're a nice guy but no thanks, once was enough.*

Might as well hang up now, but—slave to courtesy—I don't. Hear out the explanation instead, how she was involved with someone until June, likes me but isn't over him. He's older, a Commander in the Naval Reserve, a dentist, always doing Navy stuff on weekends. They just saw each other Sunday night, he stayed over, going to give it another chance.

"Well, good luck," I say when she finishes. "Give me a call if things change."

"I will," i.e., I won't.

And yet, three nights ago, there she was: her waist in my hands, her sweating back, her curses.

Neighbor across the airshaft, on the phone while she cooks, smell of garlic sauteed in sesame oil. Me slumped in the old Gimbel's chair. Familiar experience, paralysis after defeat. Don't want to see my friends, only want what I can't have.

It's Tuesday night, though. Have to call someone or I'll spend the weekend alone. Consider the list: Alan and Lori, no, too soon. Peter. Sharon. Patty. Dave and Victoria. Trouble is, it's never that satisfying getting together with friends. Each one irritating in his or her own way—just as I must be to them.

Nevertheless, down the list we go.

Peter: no, going in for foot surgery, maybe I can come visit, bring groceries, cook him dinner. Maybe.

Sharon: no, has a friend's gallery opening Friday, tickets for Twyla Tharp on Saturday, a dinner party on Sunday. Also, unwelcoming tone, I must have offended her last time, though I don't remember saying anything crass. Don't call her for a while.

Patty: no, don't even call, because Michelle always comes with her, and though I like them both, it's just too weird wishing I could date someone who's got a girlfriend of her own.

Dave and Victoria: leaving for their house in Amagansett for three weeks (right, it's August, they're both therapists) but I'm welcome to come out for the weekend. Um, well (alone with another married couple all weekend?) no, I can't, family get-together on Sunday. (World's fastest liar.) Another weekend, sure.

Pain and hardship are supposed to strengthen you, but as far as I can tell, curdled loneliness has no beneficial effect. Have sat in this chair so many times, miserably, just like this: if there's anything to be learned here, I can't seem to learn it. Instead, can feel myself turning to stone, a calcification of what was once fluid and hopeful.

Flip through the address book. Quest for a friend, a soul-mate, the perfect woman I met at a party but somehow forgot to ask out. (Pages falling out, this book is so old. Should buy a new one but then I'd have to rewrite all the names, and do you leave out the ones you haven't talked to in a year? Write them off forever?)

Suzanne.

Twirling a flower in her fingers at the wedding, a picture of heartache. We could share our loneliness, maybe rescue each other from it—like when she returned from Moscow, sick and alone. (But remember how that ended, the long escalation of desire, torture disguised as friendship, and the awful culminating moment. Don't make the same mistake twice. Don't get ambitious.)

"Hi, it's Burt."

"I was just thinking about you!"

So happy to hear my voice, unlike anyone else tonight.

"Were you thinking how charming I am, or 'What a jerk'?"

"I was hoping you'd start calling me again. I was remembering how you used to come over on the spur of the moment and we'd drink Hawaiian Punch and vodka. Remember?"

"In fact, I was just thinking about the same thing."

"I wish we could do that again."

"Well, no one's stopping us."

"How about now?"

Coy giggle, piercing my balloon, because her urgency can mean only one thing: she wants to talk about Alan.

"It's kind of late. I just took a shower."

"Pleeeeease?"

"I have to go to work in the morning."

"So do I."

"I don't know."

She says no more, just waits for me to yield.

She knows me so well.

•

Across 14th Street, cookies bouncing in the bike basket, because she never has any food to offer. Haven't come this way since a couple years ago. The question is, how humiliated should I feel about that disastrous moment? (She asked me to spend the night, because her schizophrenic neighbor stopped taking his Haldol and banged on her door screaming the night before, so I had a right to consider myself trusted, maybe her closest friend. We got along well, and the wine at the Indian restaurant gave me more nerve than usual. Also, she hadn't gone out with anyone in a long time, which she candidly confessed made her hungry for touch.

Sitting two feet away from her on her bed, leaning back against the red Ukrainian pillows, warmth of her red-tan arms radiating toward me as we laughed about childhood incidents of public vomiting: a nice connection, both of us haunted by shame for years after. Sense that we were going past old boundaries, enjoying each other, finally forgetting Alan. She had given me advice once about a woman I wanted to date who wasn't yet disentangled from an unsatisfactory boyfriend—"Don't keep worrying what *she's* thinking, do what *you* want"—and while I didn't act on the advice at the time, this seemed an even better opportunity. But I didn't work up the nerve to use the opportunity until I was on my back on the floor futon, glasses off. Couldn't even see her face as she crouched to say good night in the dark, but I clumsily, belatedly grabbed at my chance: "What if you slept here instead of there?")

It might be poignant if it were someone else's story. Since it's not, remembering is like getting a spittoon dumped on my head. Could be she didn't think me pitiful, only felt awkward, but I'll never know, because I couldn't see her face, could only see her standing up slowly and going around her desk to the bed. Lay awake most of the night, bitterly regretting while listening to the deranged neighbor shout, "Fuck you, dirty fuckers," etc. Thinking, *I would rather be him right now than me.* No mention of the misstep at breakfast, but the shame kept me from calling her, and her from calling me, ever again. Until tonight.

So how humiliated should I feel? Don't know, can't judge. Ask me again in another decade.

At 13th and A, cops have two guys with their hands against a sky-blue police car. Nearby, garbage can on fire, blackened trash. The same old Puerto Rican men as long ago, playing dominos in undershirts outside her building. One has a small poodle at his feet, leash wound around the table leg.

She's wearing culottes and a loose T-shirt, hair tied back in an elastic but working itself free around the forehead. Sheen of sweat; still hasn't bought an air-conditioner.

Friendly kiss, a fresh start, no confusing flirtation, just pals. Yet there's that baby-powder scent again, working on me.
Park the bike in the narrow hall by the door, out of the way. She gives me the only chair, one of the Ukrainian pillows softening the cane back, the other behind her on the bed. Big smile, big face.
"It's so nice to see you in my chair again."
"Those old guys are still playing dominos downstairs. Must be the longest game in history."
"They watch out for me. It's like having four extra grandfathers."
Soles of her feet just as dirty as in college. Gets up and puts a cassette in her boom box. Percussive guitars, African rhythm, no idea who this group might be. On the bohemian scale, she makes me look almost suburban.
"So what's new?" she asks as she lights a joint. This time I pass. Have a cookie instead.
"Actually, I do have news. This morning I decided to change careers."
"Wow. What would you do?"
"I don't know yet. It was an incomplete epiphany."
That laugh again. Nectar of the gods, to be thought clever by such a woman. Pillow she's leaning against has tiny mirrors sewn into it, like my sister's long-ago peasant blouse. Rusted Malayan dagger with serpentine blade on the wall. Necklaces hung on nails, from her travels in Russia, the Yucatan, India. Magazines I've never heard of lying about, plus *TV Guide* next to her computer; on the screen, a paragraph written in a Cyrillic font. Sense that she's not only cooler, but probably smarter than me.
"So what do you think I should do for a living? What profession would suit me?"
"I think you should run for Congress. You're so diligent."
Wouldn't mind bantering with her, but I'm coming up empty. Therefore, turn it around. "What about you? Do you ever sit and wonder what job would make you happy?"

"I already know: collecting unemployment. Or else—could you see me as a televangelist?"

Train of thought: No job could ever satisfy her, nor could any mate. She has always revolted against any bonds that held her, and run to whatever was furthest away. (Russia after college being the key example.) Now that both her parents are dead and her brother lives in Oregon, what connections does she have to anyone in the world? Memory of her mother and brother visiting, eating with us on yellow trays in the dining hall, a sour and unhappy woman who picked on Suzanne's brother constantly, "Why did you take so much if you're not going to eat it?" Dangerous to get close to these women.

11:15, says Felix the Clock. Books all over, half in Russian. Conversation stalled; um, ask about the manuscript on her desk. Explanation: it's a novel she's translating, by a professor who came to her as a client. Brief plot synopsis, which I lose track of because I'm staring at her tan calves, then she exhales pot smoke and a long sigh. "That was an eventful wedding," she says. "For both of us."

Here we go.

"I guess."

"You seem to have made a new friend."

"Not really. She already went back to her man in uniform."

"You could take it as a compliment. She couldn't resist you."

"Right."

What a grin she's giving me. "Want to be surprised?"

"I'm not sure."

"I think I may end up marrying Alan."

If this were a cartoon, an anvil would now fall on my head, and my eyeballs would slowly crack.

"He's so obviously unhappy. It's like someone let the air out of him. I can't see it as stealing someone else's husband—I just want to save his life."

"But."

"No one ever touched me the way he did. We could make each other so happy."

Her wide green eyes slant up at the outside corners, beautiful eyes. She terrifies me.

"I want to call him. What do you think?"

I think I'll just melt under the door, trickle down the stairs, get the hell out of here.

"I think you ought to think twice. What about his wife?"

"He was sending out some strong signals. I think he *yearns* to come back to me."

Just keep quiet. No room for mistakes here.

"But you're worried I would desert him again in the end."

"Only because you're so different from each other."

Suppressed scowl. "What drove me away in college wasn't our differences, I just dreaded marriage. You would too if you'd grown up in my family. But we're older now. I'm tired of drifting all over the planet, I want to belong somewhere."

That wavy dagger on the wall, what did the Malayans use it for? Ritual disembowelment is all that comes to mind. As in, what I would deserve if I told her what Alan said earlier tonight.

"Now you're supposed to say, 'You have my blessing.'"

Er. Um.

"Say it and we can all go back to Dunkin' Donuts together."

I'm seeing her at 20 again. Night of their engagement dinner, the fight in our kitchen, "You're so pleased with all this, it's unbearable," her teeth bared, a trapped animal.

"I'd really love to see you happy, Suzanne. I just worry about the possible consequences."

Little in her face changes—only everything. "You always were a pessimist."

"You have to admit there's a good chance it wouldn't work. Where would that leave him?"

She stabs what's left of the joint on an ash-specked seashell.

"I mean—"

"You don't have to explain yourself. Your opinion doesn't exactly come as a shock."

Her face is darkening.

"You don't know what happened when you went away, how bad it was."

"You're talking about him punching a hole in the window?"

She moves from the bed to her desk. Light from the lamp hits the mirrors in her pillow, pricking my eyes.

"I didn't think you knew."

"I asked my cousin Gerry about him when I came back from Moscow. I know I can't make up for the pain I caused him. But I did repent: by never calling him, the eight million times I've wanted to. Times when I missed him so much I couldn't breathe. The point is, I'm not indulging in an irresponsible fantasy. This time I intend to stay with him, no matter what."

I believe her. Am even beginning to wonder if she might be right, if he *could* be happier with her.

But Lori.

"There's just so much at stake." The tiny mirrors sparkle in the pillow, dazzling me. "But I guess you'll do what you want in the end, no matter what I think."

"Wrong. I won't call him without your agreement. Because I *do* care about him, and don't want to make a mistake that could hurt him. I may be a bitch at times, but I don't blithely wreck lives."

She's staring me down, angry and hopeless. Her mother's face.

Cautiously, "I wish there were something I could do to make it better."

"Just go home. You gave me your answer."

"You're sure you don't want to talk?"

"Just go, Burt."

She stands again, towering over me for one alarming moment—the dagger's in easy reach—and goes to the corner window, the furthest she can get from me without leaving her apartment.

Get out now, before her disappointment turns to rage.

•

The old guys still playing dominos, clack of white pieces. *"¡Así es!"* one croaks, *That's exactly how it is.*

Get on the bike and ride. Moving air cools my damp face, a relief.

I have been handed a power over my friends' lives that I don't want and don't know what to do with. By telling either one what the other said, I would set in motion an affair that would end in either bliss or disaster, nothing in between. If they could get together in secret, let the fever run its course without destroying Alan's marriage, I would say, Sure, go ahead. But that's not what would happen. Lori would sense the change and ask questions, and Alan would confess. That would leave him with nothing but Suzanne—in other words, walking a tightrope made of one weak thread.

But if I'm wrong and they *could* be happy together, it would be monstrous to keep them apart.

I'm not wise enough for this. All I know is, the risk is too great. Better to do nothing than cause a calamity.

Near 14th Street, a wino wobbles across First Avenue, protected by the unseen hand that keeps bums from injury. Holds a hand out to me as I pass, a self-mocking joke, *I'll ask anybody for a quarter, any time.* Unexpected humor. Startling: he's human.

Behind me, brake-squeal and thud. The wino on the ground, bleeding from the head. A stopped station wagon, and the driver, a young woman, flies out in tears. Traffic flowing around the obstruction, two cops already trotting toward them.

I have no wisdom. I know absolutely nothing.

4.

HOUR IN THE car, half-hour on the ferry, and Alan has barely said ten words all morning. Remote in his sand chair, Lucite clipboard on one thigh, writing on a yellow pad with Mont Blanc pen, while Lori huddles inside her own silence, sketching the man on the beach towel to our right. (Tan shaved head, commuter-cup of coffee in his three-ringed hand.) No fun going to the beach with a married couple when they're having problems.

Morning sun shines hard on the blown, rippling ocean, blinding white stars on olive-gray billows. In front of us, pair of Long Island nymphs on their backs, each with headphones and sunglasses, oiling arms, legs and bellies as they lie.

Lori's T-shirt catches some wind and inflates for a moment, making her arms look skinny as Minnie Mouse's. Catches me peeking at her faint, deft pencil lines—she has placed the shaved head on a platter, not what I expected—and closes the pad. "Who wants something to drink?" she asks as she opens the Igloo cooler and takes from the ice an apple that, for a half-instant, looks like a heart about to be transplanted.

"No thanks," I say, two words more than Alan.

Murmur of complaint from Lori, "Talkative, isn't he?"

Slap of his pen flat against the clipboard, retracted immediately with a semi-apologetic "I'm concentrating."

She fumbles to close the Igloo's lid, looking at neither of us. Takes off the T-shirt, goes to the water in her modest one-piece.

The only thing worse than tagging along with an unhappy couple is getting left alone with the angrier half. Obviously, he's burning up because he can't have Suzanne. Question is, does he blame me for talking him out of calling?

Probably does.

My Zen book: *If something enters your mind, let it in*

and let it out. Do not try to chase it away or stop thinking. Do not let it bother you. Do not let anything bother you.

Smell of coconut lotion, girl in a thong goes by, corkscrewed hair down past her behind. Wow.

Alan balancing a Rolodex on his left knee, considering each card in turn, then flipping. Only three names on his pad, each with a question mark.

"What are you working on?"

"Possible investors."

"Is that instead of or in addition to the loan you were applying for?"

"I don't feel like explaining."

Try not to take it personally. He's in hell.

I should put sunscreen on, but can't reach my back, am embarrassed to ask Lori, and so am doomed to burn. Better keep the T-shirt on.

One possible way to reach Alan: direct confrontation.

"You're still pretty upset, aren't you? About Suzanne, I mean."

Bullet glare, the Mesmer Eyes turned evil. "I don't need you to counsel me."

Back to his Rolodex.

Return to Zen, any page will do. *If something has entered your consciousness, then your peace is incomplete. The way to complete peace is forgetting everything.*

Another shadow passes. Nice slim calves. Except it's a guy.

Go to Lori. Just get away.

Freezing water, a bear trap closing on the ankles. Lori gazing at nothing I can see, holding her goose-pimpled arms. Far out, a boat draws a white line of wake parallel to the horizon. Closer, three girls in up to their knees smoke cigarettes.

Some mood he's in would be an appropriate comment, but she speaks first. "He hasn't—"

Mouth still open, but the voice has gotten caught.

Shakes her head, changes her mind. Wades in deeper and dives into a wave, a dolphin arc. Gone.

A whole weekend of this to look forward to.

•

Cool and damp. Big moon, but too much fog to say if it's full. Breaking waves intermittently drown the music and voices of a party on the other side of the dune. No one else on the sand, just Lori and me.

We leave our shoes and socks under the empty lifeguard chair and head east along the water's edge. Luminous white breakers, scent of fish in the air. The last foaming fringe of ocean seeps into the wet sand, a sound like effervescing soda.

Collar chafes the sunburned back of my neck. "In England they call whitecaps 'sea horses'," I say.

Weak smile, but she doesn't manage to lift her head from its slump.

A beagle trots out of the fog, steady and purposeful, along the hard wet sand. Reaching us, he slows down and falls into step at our heels. "Did you lose a dog?"

Another burdened smile.

Water rushes between my toes, cooling, tickling. Would be a heavenly night, except for all the pain.

What to talk about?

"Lori, can I ask you a question?"

"Mm?"

"Why don't you try to sell your paintings?"

Automatic answer, as if I'd asked her address. "Because I don't want everyone to see how mediocre I am."

"But you're not. *I'm* mediocre on the guitar, I know what mediocrity is. You're professional."

"I don't admire my work. It falls so far short of the things I respect."

The dog runs ahead and splashes in the water. He waits for us to catch up, then walks at Lori's side as if he were ours, Lori's and mine. The happy couple, strolling on the beach with Patches.

"You should try playing for people," she says, as if this

conversation were about me. "You don't have anything to lose. You might enjoy yourself."

I might, but only if it went this way: soloing on Open Mike day at Ruff City, with Lori in the front row of tables. Seeing me in a new light, she wishes she had a second life in which to marry me.

I should contradict her low opinion of her paintings, but don't have the will to pursue what's miles away from the point.

She scatters some foam with her toes. "Burt?"

Those hurt dark eyes.

"Uh-huh?"

"When Alan and Suzanne broke up, did he try to kill himself?"

Wo. "Where did that come from?"

"I overheard someone gossiping at the wedding."

"Well." Careful now. Examine each word for possible consequences. "No one knows what really happened, only him. He says it was an accident, he cut himself on a broken window." Though I've always doubted that you could break a pane of glass by simply reaching for something on the other side.

"Did he go to the hospital?"

"Just overnight."

"And did you keep an eye on him afterwards?"

"A little. I slept on the floor of his room for a couple nights. The doctor told Alan it was just in case he felt weak and needed help."

Her voice is small and thin. "You're a good friend. A lifeguard."

Yelp of a nervous laugh, because right now all I want to do is hold my good friend's wife in my arms.

The crash of waves has grown louder in our silence. Huge, powerful ocean: easy to forget, when you're busily doing tasks in the city, that anything can be so grand.

"I'm afraid of what's happening," she says, a bright dot of moon in each moist eye. "He pulls away when I touch him. He's been dissatisfied with me ever since he saw her."

"He'll calm down. All you have to do is stick it out."

"I'm afraid he's having an affair with her."

As if to make this ridiculous, the beagle gazes up mournfully at us.

"No. If that's what's bothering you, I'm glad you told me, because now I can reassure you. He's just confused, he's off-balance—we talked about it. You're right that seeing her stirred up memories, but he knows better than to act on them. She made him miserable, he hasn't forgotten that."

Her head still hanging low, her hand inches from mine. Put my arm around her? No, mixed motives, don't.

"I feel like I'm falling," she says, "like there's no ground underneath me."

"You're not. You'll be fine."

Role reversal: tight-lipped Lori bares her soul, and what does Burt do? Tells her to clamp down.

Someone has built a bonfire up ahead, a good destination, but suddenly it has gotten late, too late to keep walking. We stop a hundred yards short of the fire, and let the ocean wash our feet, draw the sand out from under our heels. No houses in sight, only the fog and waves and us.

The dog runs on ahead, done with us. A pang—missing him.

"We should head back," I murmur. She doesn't disagree.

At each lifeguard chair, we seek our shoes. Chair after chair after chair. Didn't realize we came this far.

Not a word passes between us, but at least she seems less agitated than before. At the wooden stairs over the dune, she leans on the railing to put her sandals back on, while I wish she had leaned on me instead.

Her parents' beach house: red clapboard, white trim. Alan pacing slowly in the front window, his back to us. He has the old black phone in his hand, his head bent, absorbed in the call. Glances out the front window, sees us under the yellow porchlight, and straightens instantly.

Uh-oh.

Lori, eyes downcast, didn't see. A temporary mercy.
The blood has deserted my head. I was wrong. For the millionth time.
Oh Lori. If I could swim out and save you, I would.

•

The point of the Flatiron Building. I should spot Suzanne no matter which side she comes out of. Irritable after-work crowds swarming by me, bad place to loiter. There's still time to walk away, before I get myself tangled in barbed wire. That's what a wise man would do.

Nevertheless, here I remain. The opposite of wise.

There she goes, denim jacket with red rose sewn on the back, long splashy skirt. With her, a girlfriend with a platinum blond crew-cut, a teenager.

Catch up with them. Glimpse from the side her wide grin, which gives me the answer I came for. If she's smiling, then they're having an affair. No need to speak to her.

(By now they must have told their respective stories about longing for each other and confiding in Burt. So, Alan knows I kept her desire secret from him. That's why he froze me out all weekend at Fire Island. He'll never forgive me.)

"Suzanne."

A confused smile serves as a screen behind which to decide whether to handle me as enemy or ally.

"Burt! Are you lurking?"

I have no comeback.

"This is Rima, my co-worker. Speak slowly, she's just learning English."

The girl (red lipstick, black eye-makeup) pouts.

"How are you, Rima?"

Not a word, not a twitch, just some speed-Russian with Suzanne, after which she heads west.

Suzanne and I turn east, toward her neighborhood, away from mine. She's still smiling, but has nothing to say to me. Or, nothing she's willing to say aloud.

"You look happier than last time," say I.
"I have a friend in the Lord?"
"No, I don't think that's it."
"I greet each day with a big joyful smile?"
"Nope."
"Oh Burt, can't a person be happy without your worrying about it?"
"I guess not."
"I'd love to tell you my secrets, but I'm not allowed. Keep asking questions, though, it's fun."
"You're not planning to quietly disapear with anyone, are you?"
"No, and why are you so glum? Cheer up, everybody's happy."

Right. Everybody.

At Broadway, a shuttered store suddenly has no one in front of it, because Alan has fled, briefcase in left hand, mylar-wrapped roses in right. A dozen, I'd say.

"Whoops," Suzanne giggles.

"Did I thwart something?"

"Must have been a surprise. We didn't have plans."

She has bloomed, her smile wider than ever, because now her happiness has a witness.

"I guess you might say," reciting the words she once taught me, *"U nivo stayit."* He has a hard-on.

Hilarity, squeezes my arm. "He called me at work the day after you came over. We walked home together. I was afraid to ask him up, in case he refused, so we talked downstairs for an hour, across the street from the domino guys."

"As if he could ever have refused you."

"I didn't know. Neither of us knew what the other one was thinking. It seemed like forever before he touched me—just like freshman year."

Easy to picture the scene, and to envy. "Sounds romantic."

"He's so sweet, and so passionate. I keep waiting for things to settle down, but they don't."

Enough. "I guess I should say congratulations."

"In college we were too young to appreciate what we had. We're like angels flying in the clouds, doing what we were made to do. I don't care if I sound sappy." Champagne laughter. "I've said to myself, 'If years of misery were the price for getting him back, then it was worth the price.'"

Some skateboarders practicing stunts at Union Square, going down a wooden ramp and off a lip: flying, if only briefly. Would-be angels. I can't disapprove of Suzanne, because I would do the same thing if I had the chance.

"I don't think Alan will ever forgive me for not telling him what you said."

"You're wrong. A happy person is a generous person."

Her reassurance sends tingles up the back of my neck, and overcomes my resistance. They're not doing wrong, they're doing what they must. Lori is unfortunate, true, but it's like the hawk eating the field mouse. You can't fight the laws of nature.

•

Imagine it. What they have—what I want.

Suzanne's apartment, after work. In her peach undershirt with spaghetti straps, the one she used to wear under an open Hawaiian shirt, breasts defined by the stretched cotton ribs. She's lounging on her bed among the pillows with the tiny mirrors. He's facing her in the chair, a game they play, neither allowed to touch the other for five full minutes. Alan solemn with desire. She says, "Time," a minute early, and he crosses to the bed in a single step. She unties his tie and tosses it over the chair. (How does he erase the perfume she will leave on his shirt? Ignore that, don't get distracted.) He slides one hand under the flimsy shirt, up the underside of one breast. Squeezes the nipple between two fingers until it hardens, then he lifts the shirt and takes the brown thimble in his lips.

This is too tame, I'm not getting it right. Hard to imagine utopia when you've only seen New York—but try. Reach for it.

Her smirk dissolves as he kisses her breasts. Her fingernails scratch his scalp as he unzips her cutoffs and kisses the warm skin in the V between the zipper's teeth. He pulls down cutoffs and panties at once, kisses lower and lower. Now she's crying, sobs you would never have expected from one so sardonic. This is what excites him more than anything else in the world, her ascent from wit to sobs, his ability to lift her all the way to screams.

And now, while she recovers her breath, he strips off shirt and pants and comes back home, back where he belongs, after seven years of exile. But the feeling of him inside her awakens her again, so he slows down, moves in ways that move her. A heavenly reward, to see her shake and sob in his hands, until she lets loose a groan the domino-players must hear down in the street. *Now* he can move for himself, hunched over and kissing those huge brown nipples, left then right then both pushed together.

Except, I can't believe in this. It's fantasy, more perfect than even they can have.

Adjust it, then. Let it be me—with Lori, on *my* bed. Still wounded by divorce, she asks me with her eyes never to betray her, because she couldn't survive it a second time. Makes me turn the light out before undressing. Naked, she sits across my lap on the couch, delicate as a candle-flame in a draft, and we kiss softly in the dark, a way you wouldn't kiss Suzanne. Lori, the fragile one.

This I can imagine.

And more than imagine. It's possible I could *have* her. For real, after all these years.

(White-faced fear. Like the vice-president who learns the president has just been shot.)

•

Telephone ringing. Swing guitar around behind me so the pegs don't hit the wall. (Is it Alan, calling to tell me off?)

"Hello?"

"Hi Burt."

Lori. Small voice submerged in cordless phone static, but I can hear trouble, clear as a bell.

"How's it going?" I ask.

"All right. What are you doing today?"

"There's a bar with an open mike, I was going to sign up. Taking your advice."

"You're going to play guitar at a bar?"

"Uh-huh. I was just working on my solo. Hopefully I won't humiliate myself too badly. And if I do, at least no one there knows me." I.e., Don't ask to come.

"I'd love to see you play. Would you mind?"

"I'm extremely self-conscious about this. My nerves are, *dzzzzzz*."

In her silence, the phone line picks up some far-away country music. Doinky guitar, carefree, as if there were no such thing as trouble.

"Lori?"

"It's okay." Squeak on the letter *K*. She's bad off.

"Maybe it would be good if you came. You could clap and cheer."

No answer.

"Lori? I'd *like* you to come. Would you?"

Limply, "All right."

I know that sound. When you ask for help and it comes a little too late, too grudgingly, and you have to go ahead and accept it, though what you really want is to curl up in the dark and sleep for the next hundred years.

"Maybe we can get drunk afterwards, forget our problems."

"Mm."

Give up. Too late. Just do better from now on.

•

There she is, next to the rusted steel door. Gnawing a thumbnail, something I've never seen her do. Sleeveless white dress, she must have assumed it was some kind of nightclub, despite the daylight; dress looks awful on her, arms and legs sticking out like pipe-cleaners. How much weight can a person lose in a month?

"Hi," calm as I can manage.

"Hi." Half-smile, cancelled by the worry crease between her eyebrows.

Dark inside, A/C on full blast, hardly anyone here. Chunky blonde girl in too-tight mini-dress and cowboy boots, drunk in her black boyfriend's muscular arms. By the cigarette machine, two Japanese students with shaved-off sideburns, shooting pool. Bartender's long hair covers much of a flesh-tone neckbrace.

"There are usually more people."

Tucks her lips in, a silent *Mm*.

B. Roy Barkley and the Boys, the house band, meander to their places, take up their instruments. B. Roy (a former junkie, I assume: tired eyes, gray skin with bones showing through, a skull face) mumbling ironic words I can't quite make out, while the drummer whisks his cymbal as in cool jazz, a joke. "Go, Daddy-o," says B. Roy. Mocking, always mocking. Does anyone talk straight any more?

"Are your shoulders cold?"

"No. Are you nervous?"

I'd forgotten, until she reminded me. "Yes."

The looseleaf sign-up sheet, beer-wet already, only has one name on it. If I sign up now, I'll go on stage too soon. Wish Lori weren't here, so I could skip out unnoticed. Instead, I print my name, heart thumping like a funeral drum.

B. Roy, laid back almost to the point of sleep, says, "Are you ready to roll?" then *wham,* amplified blues, the floor shakes. Painfully loud but that helps, hard to think of anything else with this sound hammering you in the face. Even Lori has looked up from her lap, noticing something outside her gloom.

"Something to drink?" I ask in her ear. She opens her purse—I close it—and says, "A margarita." Her bar drink, I remember from our pre-Alan dates.

Daylight from the front window falls sidewise over the shoulders of the many bottles, turning them silver. Lori facing the band, but seeing something beyond them, something haunting, the image of her fear.

She's hugging herself when I get back from the bar. Put the two glasses down on the wobbly table, press a damp hand to her shoulder. She's shaking. In her ear, "Tell me what's wrong. What happened?"

She doesn't look at me.

"Tell me."

Quick shake of the head, nothing more.

B. Roy, off-duty during the keyboard solo, takes a swig from his flask and dances with his guitar as if it were a woman, one arm around the body, the other hand high on the neck. Lori sips her drink and stares at the tarnished nickel nailed to the tabletop. Burt left alone with his stage fright. (Remember the fantasy: playing onstage, I win Lori's love. And here we are, all the pieces present, but everything jumbled, mangled, hopeless.)

"Okay," B. Roy says, "we're gonna bring some folks up." He holds the sign-up sheet at arm's length under the spotlight, a far-sighted old man. "I know you've been waiting on the edges of your stools for . . . Toshi."

One of the pool players unzips a soft leather case and takes out a blonde Telecaster like mine, except shiny-new and therefore less cool. Has to tune up, with keyboard help. Meanwhile, bass man plays "Funiculi, Funicula," musical thumb-twiddling, which pumps me full of dread that my guitar will require on-stage tuning too, that I will look as dumb as Toshi does. (Shameful: worrying how ten dissolute strangers will judge me, while Lori's life falls apart. Nevertheless, can't stop worrying.)

The song is "Why I Sing the Blues." Toshi discreet on rhythm, until B. Roy hands him the solo and then, I'm doomed, he's a virtuoso. Chuck Berry double-stops, beautiful stinging accents, nice flutter effect too. If not for Lori, I'd run for my life.

Holding her drink in two hands, light glinting prettily

off the rim, unnoticed by her. Bloodshot, hopeless eyes. Lips drawn with such a fine pen, not fleshy like Suzanne's.
"Next up, we got . . . lookie here, it's Burt. Come on, man, get up here. If you're any good, maybe you and me'll start a new band, 'The Burts'."
Stand up, take guitar from its case. Don't move too fast, stay cool, don't stumble. Toshi pulling out his patch cord, which means I must take mine up with me. "Good luck," from pale Lori, a valiant effort.
Many wires to trip over, but caution protects me. Patch in, play an E chord, adjust volume on guitar. "This is in F," B. Roy tells me off-mike, then gives a baton-like jerk of the head, "If you ever—change your mi-ind . . . about leaving, leaving me behind..."
Okay, a standard, I can do this. Join on rhythm, watch my left hand. Haven't played with anyone since college, all I remember is, don't play any licks while he's singing, wait for the pauses between the lines. Strap lies heavy across my shoulder, dense ash wood, a burden. Thick line of bass thumping up through my sneaker-soles, and there, now I can hear it, my guitar behind the other instruments. Part of the band.
"Show us what you got, Brother Burt," he says through the mike.
Concentrate, don't get reckless or cocky. Work my way up the neck, just as I practiced. Sounds pretty good, melodic, smooth, simple, though no telling what the audience thinks. Bend from 15th fret to 17th, then one last ringing vibrato and it's over. Not a single mistake.
Three or four people applaud as I go back to rhythm. (Did they clap more for Toshi? Can't remember now.) Lori clapping too, smiling for me, while tears drip from her eyes.
Can't help her now, I've got my own troubles. Two more solos to get through, for which I stupidly didn't prepare.
An old guitar-tip: make up words to go with the notes, for improved phrasing. *Lori . . . I don't know . . . don't know*

how or what to do for you . . . sweet woman, wish I knew, I'd rescue you, yes I would, yes I would, yes I would . . .

This time five or six people clap. My popularity is spreading.

Last solo. "Go wild," B. Roy says, and despite misgivings, I obey. Close my eyes like he does, forget about fingering patterns, search for new sounds in the dark. Two guys howl like wolves; it's working, rougher and better phrases are coming out than ever before. Fantastic!

Wait—no. Try again—no. Fumbling, lost. What key are we in?

Stop and follow the chord progression until I find my way back. Should have known better, I'm not at this level. Idiot, to forget my limits.

"You played some nice things," B. Roy says quietly as the next guy comes up. Pull my cord from the amp, hands trembling. Somebody slaps my back, "All right!" and the mistakes no longer matter. Want to climb up the side of the World Trade Center, throw a javelin across the Hudson.

Lori small in her seat, "You were great," she says, eyes still wet, but we'll fix that. Take her outside, into the air and light. Lift her.

Guitar back in its case, people watching me as if I were a celebrity. "Let's leave," I say into her ear, which it's hard to keep from kissing.

Out past the band, B. Roy already into the next song, kid with a kerchief around his forehead in my place. I've sweated through my shirt, cold in the A/C, didn't notice until now.

Daylight, warm sun. The steel door swings shut behind us, sealing off most of the music. Want to hug her—to comfort her, and share this joy—but she's shielding her eyes from the light, that acute elbow keeping me away.

"Let's do something, go somewhere, have fun."

"I" is all she says, and then she's holding me, arms circling my arms, face pressed against my shoulder, holding on tight and sobbing so hard that my flesh shakes. "Let me put this down," guitar case on sidewalk, then my hands on her back. She's so thin, so small. Stroke her fine hair and she clings even tighter, digging for some kernel of comfort, crying loud enough for everyone on the block to hear. Lori, who has never exposed a single strand of sadness before.

Warm trickle down my neck, and pale scalp visible on either side of her part: her hair is so thin. Want to take care of her, protect her.

"Ssssh, it'll be all right."

"I heard him—" But instead of finishing, she looks up at me. "You know?"

"I just found out this week."

Comes back into my embrace. "He sounded so intimate with her. I never felt so alone before."

"You're not alone. You're not." One hand stroking her hair.

She presses closer, no longer sobbing. Stays buried against me, holding on. It's good to give comfort. No need to go anywhere else.

5.

ALAN DRIVING, HAGGARD and grim, like the hero of a movie who must shoot his friend in the head before the night's over. I'm not exactly bubbly either. There are only two reasons why he would have invited me to a Yankee game: either Suzanne twisted his arm, coerced him to make up with me, or else he intends to tell me off. Either way, not an evening to look forward to.

Jet rising from LaGuardia catches a glint from the just-set sun. 6:49 in green digits on the dashboard clock; we should reach the stadium in time to see batting practice. But it's hard to get excited about baseball right now.

Too long a silence. Break it.

"Did you read about the crazy kid at the zoo? With the polar bear?"

"Mm-hm."

Gnaws his thumbnail like Lori outside the bar. *That's* where she learned it.

"I don't see why they had to kill the bear, he was just doing what animals do. Unless they think it'll deter the other bears."

He touches the CD-player and lush classical strings pour from the doors. Far cry from the R&B he used to love. "The police said they thought there was a second kid in there."

"Ah."

The FDR divides, we go right, the road swoops up and over, and bam! we're right in the tail end of a traffic jam. Speedometer needle falls counterclockwise like the altimeter of a plane in a nosedive. "I don't *believe* this," mutters Alan. Looks for a lane to change to, but there is none.

Bomb of a Buick squeals to a stop alongside us. Driver, in a Yankee cap, glowers at me as if I made the traffic.

"So we miss an inning or two. It's not a big deal."

Dyspeptic frown, deep creases from nostrils to mouth-corners. "I don't have the tickets yet."

"I thought you said you did."

"I have to look for a scalper."

That could cost a fortune: the Yanks may clinch the American League East tonight. "What do they get, fifty bucks a ticket?"

"I'll be lucky if I can talk my way down to a hundred."

I was planning to pay him back for mine. Now what?

"There's something I have to tell you," he says.

Heart throbs thickly. Just hear him out. "Uh-huh."

He keeps his eyes on the road, massages the middle of his forehead with left hand. "I invited someone else to the game. My cousin David. You met him once, we played softball with him and his friends."

I remember: David Grubler. The one who made us wear yarmulkes with bobby pins so we wouldn't embarrass him in front of his friends. The one who yelled, "Shmuck!" when I threw from left field to 3rd instead of 2nd, missing a possible put-out.

"He owns four kosher restaurants now, he's a millionaire. If he rents my vacant coffee shop on Fulton Street, that would solve half my problems."

Which raises the question, What am I doing here?

"Are you going to ask him about it tonight?"

"Only if it feels right. I don't want to push too hard."

"Hm."

Next to us, a white-haired woman in a white Cadillac, steering wheel covered with white fleece. Would normally point out such a comic sight and share a snicker, but don't feel like it right now.

Though I haven't asked, he elaborates. "There's a loan I may need to pay back early."

"The balloon mortgage, I remember."

"No, this is something else. A private loan."

Glances over at me, an uncertain look. I'm too annoyed to give sympathy. What's a private loan anyway? From friend or family, he must mean. Yes: Lori's father lent him some huge sum way back, that's how he bought his first building.

He'll have to give the money back. He wanted to tell me—to acknowledge his affair.
No longer looking my way.
"Yes, a private loan, and?"
"I need your help tonight."
"Tell me what to do."
"I have to make a good impression, it's extremely important to me. Don't joke around with him. Let me do the talking. He comes from a different world."
I see. A good impression requires that I keep my mouth shut.
"Wouldn't you be better off alone with him?"
"I want it to seem casual, just a night at the ballgame. I may not even mention business."
He goes back to gnawing his thumbnail. I was expecting an apologetic P. S., *I know it's a weird favor to ask,* some recognition of the insult in his request, but all he says is, "Come on, *move,*" to the cars in front of us.
The colon on the dashboard clock blinks once per second. A steady pulse, something to hold onto. Time will pass. Just watch the clock.

•

"Are they gonna do it tonight?" asks a fool with greasy hair and scorecard. A pretzel-chewer replies, "No more kidding around."
Fans swarming through the gates, Alan still hunting for a scalper over by the El. I'm searching for a chubby guy in a yarmulke, without confidence that I'll recognize him, since he'll be surrounded by a hundred other people who arranged to meet their friends by the giant bat—which really looks more like a naval smokestack, gray and welded. Seven minutes to game time. Recording plays over the loudspeakers for the dozenth time, *The buying or selling of tickets in the area outside the stadium, including the parking lot, is a violation of law.* Maybe the cops have hauled Alan away. Amusing thought.

Nope, here he comes, car radio in hand. "I couldn't get box seats, we're up in the loge."
No comment required. Practice keeping silent.
Out of the back of a pale gray Lincoln Town Car climbs a slob, white shirt pulling out of his stiff dark jeans. And a bright-white yarmulke.
"Dave!" Alan shoots one arm straight up.
Grubler spots Alan, says something to his chauffeur, waddles toward us.
"They should make gas ten dollars a gallon so people would stay off the roads," he says, and turns Alan's handshake into a hug. *(I revere family. The rest of the world, however, can go to hell.)*
"We just got here ourselves. Remember my college roommate, Burt?"
I offer my hand, and he shakes it without looking at me. Blue ink smeared on some of his fingers, which, oddly, have the most perfectly trimmed, gleaming nails I've ever seen.
"What kind of seats are we in?" he asks Alan as we head toward the gate.
"There was a mixup. My connection didn't come through."
Philosophical shrug. "C'est la vie."
Up the ramps, up the escalator, through the bleak concrete innards of the stadium. Each rectangular portal, though, gives us a glimpse of paradise: spring-green grass, players in clean white uniforms sprinting here and there. Mower-stripes criss-cross the outfield, while high above, a bank of lights makes me squint. "*Ice* cream here," a woman sings, Caribbean patois audible in the three words. Sea of voices, spirit of mass anticipation. Grandeur, encouraging me to rise above my resentment.
We're over third base, a square white pillow, clean as hospital linen. In front of us, broken-nosed Puerto Rican father and wide-eyed son with a righty's mitt on his right (i.e., wrong) hand. At my side, a solitary old beer-guzzler, thick gray hair low over red face, crooning, "Tonight, tonight." Maybe 20% of the fans have on Yankee caps, that

venerable logo, the crossed *N* and *Y*, almost a pictograph. Full spectrum of skin here, from Irish paler-than-me to blackest black.

Organ fanfare as the Yanks take the field. Fierce roar of appreciation.

"I miss the girders," Grubler says. "This was still an old-time stadium when I was a kid. The House that Ruth Built."

"I remember your room. You had a Yankee pennant and that ball on a gold pedestal with Mickey Mantle's autograph." Alan's accent more Jewish than usual; must be the gravitational force of Grubler's money.

Announcer on the P. A., "And now, Robert Merrill will sing our national anthem."

"I thought he was dead," I murmur to Alan as we rise.

"It's not live, it's a tape."

Then it's *really* not live, I want to say but don't. Must not display whimsy in front of the millionaire.

People putting hands over their hearts, many even singing, as if this were 1945. Alan and I maintain respectful stillness, hands crossed over groins, but Grubler says, "You have to give New York credit. Where else can fifty-six thousand people get drunk and not kill each other?"

My beer-guzzling neighbor gives him a glare, *You in da yommica, sing or shut ya face.*

The applause starts on *land of the free* and builds to wild cheering by the word *brave*. People pointing to the broadcasters' booth, and there's Robert Merrill in a pink shirt, waving, apparently still alive. As we sit down and settle in, Grubler says, "You want to hear something tragic? This is the first game I've been to all season. Fucking restaurant business."

"If I could do what you've done," Alan says, "I'd trade in all of my buildings in three seconds."

"You don't know. It's a nightmare that never ends. My produce man had a stroke last month, now his kids are running the business and we have to send back every third crate."

"Anything beats tenants. I have people who pay 200 a month, which doesn't even cover the heating, and then they leave their garbage in the hall and complain to the City about unsanitary conditions."

Grubler studying the back of one hand, those shining nails. "I told you a long time ago, low-income means problems."

"I've learned my lesson. The next building I buy will be in Manhattan, luxury apartments."

Grubler still staring at his hand. "A strange thing happened to me today. I went and had a manicure to make Ellen happy, she's been telling me for years how disgusting my nails are. So what happens? The girl jabs me with the cuticle-cutters, and a drop of blood comes out. They swear they sterilize, but what does that mean, a tray of alcohol? Now my life depends on who sat in the seat before me. All because my wife doesn't like my fingernails."

Alan gives a choked laugh, which could be passed off as a cough if Grubler didn't mean to be funny. Grubler opens his program; Alan does the same.

Since I'm not welcome, might as well watch the game. One guy's already flied out, and the new batter has the weirdest stance I ever saw, bat hanging down his back, left leg opened toward third base. Chops one past the pitcher, and the shortstop drops down like a lanky cat, all elbows and knees, glove in the dirt, sucks that ball up sweetly into his glove, then whips it over to first, so perfect it looks easy. I will never do anything as well as he did that.

"Burt has an interesting job," Alan says. "He gets grants for a literacy group, so they can help more people."

"Our shul has a fundraiser. Every year he comes to my house and shows off that he knows my kids' names. He literally has the index card sticking out of his pocket."

If I can't talk, don't even listen.

Alan calls over a beer vendor—cups caged in a rack of rods, foam sloshing under the lids—and asks Grubler, "Do you drink beer?" In other words, Is it kosher?

"Not often enough," Grubler says, so Alan buys three, $9.75, and holds a twenty out past my face.

"The best money is in the beer," Grubler explains while the guy hands Alan his change. "Souvenirs are the lowest. The vendors have a hierarchy."

Jimmy Key strikes out the third Chicago batter, gets an explosive roar. Grubler grumbles about Yankee weaknesses (no bullpen, slow on the basepaths) while Alan nods, the subordinate, the disciple—as if he didn't know all this and more. It's grotesque.

The Yanks at bat. Boggs flies out, Dion James steps up to the plate. Fouls into the seats near us, and a dozen people dive for the ball. Next pitch, he cracks a solid line drive down the middle, right over the ump in short center. The organ plays *Hal-lelujah, hallelujah,* and what's this, an old familiar tingle creeps up my spine: the thrill of fandom.

Grubler stops a Chinese peanut kid, "Let me see a bag," checks for a kosher seal, buys two. Opens one, stashes the other in his shirt pocket.

When Tartabull comes to the plate, the P.A. plays the noisy clap-clap *stomp* tape, and the fans join in, CLAP CLAP STOMP, CLAP CLAP *STOMP*. The kid in front of us looks to his father for the go-ahead (guy must be a tyrant at home) and the father claps and stomps to show it's okay. The boy claps hand against mitt and shifts down in his seat to reach the concrete with one sneaker.

No score in this inning or the next. Grubler, chewing peanuts and dropping the broken shells at our feet, recites the retired numbers on the outfield monuments with his eyes closed, *4, 3, 5, 7, 37, 8, 8.* (I know Ruth and DiMaggio, the rest of the numbers mean nothing to me.) High foul ball into the grandstands by first base, and a guy rises half out of his seat with a beer, catches it effortlessly in his bare left hand, sits down again, gets an ovation. "Easy catch," says Grubler, "the ball was at its apogee."

Ooo, ten-dollar word. Come on, Alan, make your pitch, get it over with.

The novelty of the game has already worn off. Mob

taunts the Yankee catcher, who hasn't hit in the last ten games. Roll of toilet paper unfurls from the grandstand and snakes in the chilly breeze. They have as much mercy as a guillotine. (As if any of them could hit a major league pitch. It's like cabdrivers calling the president a moron.) Swing and a miss, hoots from all around. "Close your eyes, maybe you'll get lucky," my red-faced neighbor caws, and the little kid looks back at him, confused—why are these people booing a *Yankee?* But his father laughs too, so it must be all right. (My theory: They can't get laid, so their semen goes rancid and reacts with beer to produce an explosive gas, the fart-like language of assholes.)

Strikeout, and the boy laughs with the men.

As if to punish the cruel New Yorkers, God gives the White Sox two runs in the next inning. Alan leans forward, elbows on knees, then catches himself looking anxious and leans back again. Shoving match between some Sock and Gallego at second, with shouted encouragements from the stands, "Kick his ass, Mike." Have to admit, since I can't spit in Grubler's face, I wouldn't mind seeing someone else throw a punch. And here we go, the Sock takes a swing and two Yankees come tearing out of the dugout. Now twenty men are writhing together around second base, the umps yelling loud enough to hear, "Get back in your dugouts! Get back in your dugouts!"

Something splats a few rows behind us, spilled beer from the next tier up. Two guys duking it out at the railing. This is almost as classy as a hockey game.

Calm returns, though—even boredom. On the scoreboard, *Happy Anniversary to Betty and Pat Konitsiotis.* Which reminds me of Alan and Lori, who may never have another anniversary, and Suzanne, and the loan Alan will have to repay. He's risking his business to be with her. No matter what else you say, you have to admire his guts.

While the men of the grounds crew drag the mats around the arc of infield dirt, Alan asks me to watch his car radio and squeezes past my knees, call of nature. I have no problem ignoring Grubler as he has ignored me, except that

this is a chance to help Alan, put in a good word for him, something he can't say on his own behalf.
Choose the words carefully. *He's a good guy, Alan.* (Lame.) *He'll be richer than you in ten years.* (Yeah, right.) *Your cousin works harder than anyone I know.* (No, makes him sound sweaty and desperate.)
Give up. Better silence than fiasco.
"Excuse me," says Grubler, leaning my way.
"Uh-huh?"
"I noticed you aren't drinking that beer. If you don't want it..."
Hand it across the empty blue seat. The manicured fingernails take it away.

2-2, top of the 8th, missed a home run when I went to the bathroom. Cold out here, should have brought a sweatshirt. While I rub my arms, the Puerto Rican father drips sweat, dying from the suspense, "Come on, come on, get it over with." Seems Alan won't be making his pitch tonight.
The crowd, well-lubricated by now, sings, "Let's go, Jim-my, let's go." Jimmy Key winds up, watching the runner on first, and throws a strike, bringing down a massive war whoop. Next pitch, broken-bat grounder to second, Gallego makes the catch, twists left, whips the ball to Mattingly. YER OUT, screams the scoreboard.
Grubler rocking forward and back in his seat, so immersed in the game that Alan scarcely dares to speak. "Hang tough, Jimmy," Grubler mutters.
Next batter is Bo Jackson, and the crowd starts cheering, which I don't understand. "The Tigers just went ahead of Toronto," says a guy across the aisle, black transistor radio at his ear, watching the game through a single frameless eyeglass lens. (What's he doing buying a loge ticket when he can't even afford glasses? Put *that* on *Unsolved Mysteries.*) And there's what everyone's cheering, on the side scoreboard: DET 3 TOR 1. The Yanks will clinch if either they win or Toronto loses. The title is almost theirs.
Applause for Key as he gets out of the inning. First up

for the Yanks, Dion James: long drive to right, and I scream along with everyone else, "*Yeah!*" as he takes first base. Mattingly draws a walk, Tartabull comes up, the organ goes, *Doo-doo-doo-*DOO*, doo* doo! and the crowd answers, "*CHARGE.*" At 3 and 1, Tartabull breaks the rules and swings beautifully, *CRACK,* long ball to right center, bounces over the fence for a ground-rule double. Ump motions Mattingly back to third but James scores, we're ahead, and the whole stadium is bellowing, *Yeah! Yeah! Yeah!*

Interruption. A man and a woman run into left field and spread a banner, *1000s of NYERS ARE HUNGRY.* Boos, hisses, laughter. "I'm pretty hungry myself," says someone behind us, and now the two are nabbed by a security guard, no three, no five security guards, black hands gripping white arms. The guards hustle them out through the Sox dugout.

"That's what happens when you let Mets fans in," I say.

Grubler: "They look more like fundraisers to me."

The Grubler wit. I'm skewered.

Between us, a *sssss,* Alan chuckling through his teeth. Tried to hold it in but couldn't.

Just sit. Watch the batter swing, see the outfielder run. Listen to the cheers rise and then fall when the glove closes around the ball. This constriction in the throat will pass; so will the burning in the face. Smell the hot dog and mustard in front of us, see the peanut shells at our feet. Look at no one, look only at what's far away, the brilliant flecks of T-shirt color, turquoise, orange, purple. The world torn into confetti.

This happened once before: no air to breathe because Alan took all the air away. In his old car, the Monza, driving up to school in a blizzard. Six hours of crawling, Suzanne and him in front, me in the back, the car skidding whenever he went above five miles an hour. Dusk, and the fear of getting snowed in overnight, stranded on the highway. Wondering whether you could freeze to death that way. No cars in front of us after a while, hard to see the road. He almost drove into a tree, but braked, steered and skidded, got past it with maybe three inches to spare. Couple miles later, another tree came into view and I, to pierce the tension, said, "Want to try that tree maneuver again?" He snapped, "I wouldn't criticize if I drove like you." Which hit me like a falling rock. Never expected him to expose the truth, that beneath his affection and playfulness, he disdained me. The exact thing I had feared since the day we met, that football game behind Otsego Hall, when he passed to me, I dropped the ball, and he rolled his eyes.

No more. Get up and take the train home.

Can't move, though. Because walking away would mean admitting the hurt, a shameful thing.

Resolved: Never again will I play sidekick. Loathsome, humiliating role.

As of tonight, our friendship is over.

Top of the ninth. Security guards lined up facing the crowds in the box seats, ready to use fists and nightsticks to keep the celebration off the field.

"You know," Alan says to Grubler, "I'd really love for you to come look at my Fulton Street building."

"Why, for its historical interest?" Smirking, because he can smell a pitch a mile away.

"No, I really think you'd be interested. There's a restaurant space that's vacant, and this is a block that gets an amazing amount of pedestrian traffic."

"I know the neighborhood. Unfortunately, not many of those pedestrians eat kosher. Maybe if I opened a jerk chicken place."

"Well, I think the building might interest you in other ways. It's two blocks from a park, forty apartments, very solid mechanically." (Drab brown box, belongs in a housing project.) "The rent roll was two hundred thousand when I bought it, but I can raise it twenty percent with a little cosmetic work. The problem is, I'm in a situation where one of my investors may pull out his money, he needs it for personal reasons. If he pulls out, I'll have to sell, because it's the easiest one of my buildings to turn around, but I don't want to sell until the market improves. All I really need is a simple loan. I could give a very fair return."

Waits for a response, not long enough to get one. Tries again. "Or, we could work out an equity participation."

Grubler breaks a shell, drops one of the nuts in his mouth, chews. "I have a rule, based on experience. Never get involved in anything you don't control. I assume you don't want me controlling your buildings. Why don't you just go to a bank?"

Quiet, because he has failed. "I may have to."

"Look, I want to help you. Tell you what I'll do. Invite me to your office and I'll look over your books, see if I can make suggestions. You may be underfinanced, that's a common problem. Second, a tip in case you don't know it: take every building you own and convert space so the majority of your square footage is residential. That takes you from the worst tax status to almost the best. Third, let me ask a personal question. When was the last time you went to shul?"

"The day before my wedding."

Grimace, "At least you're honest. Okay, my advice to you is, join a shul and get active. It'll be good for your soul, and you'll enjoy yourself. So tell me you'll go, make me feel better."

From his inside jacket pocket, Alan takes an electronic organizer, size of a checkbook. Types with one finger, and the word *synagogue* spills out on the flat gray screen. As he's typing, a Sox batter sends a shot down the first base line—men on second and third, could cost New York the game—but Mattingly dives, snares it in his huge lobster-claw glove. Pandemonium: three outs, the Yankees have won the East.

Infielders pile onto the pitcher, outfielders run in too. Around us, plastic horns, wails, shrieks. The Puerto Rican father puts his son on his shoulders, shakes all of our hands, tells the boy to do the same. The rosy drunk sings, "Fly me to the moon, and let me float among the stars." Grubler shaking hands all around while Alan and I stand silently, a hole in the merriment. The car radio hangs from his hand like a shriveled attaché case. "I'm going down to look for my car, beat some of the traffic," Grubler says. "Bring Lori to one of my restaurants some time, you'll be my guest."

I move out into the aisle to let him by. Three bare-chested teenagers stagger past us, down the concrete steps, and Grubler follows them. The white yarmulke recedes into the revelry.

I could walk away now. The slap in the face that he deserves.

But I don't.

•

Middle-aged prostitute waits for business on a dark street of cobblestones. Red tail lights block our way. No music in the car this time, except the happy honking from outside.

Onto the highway, past dark cranes and bridges. Across the river in Manhattan, apartment buildings like a prison complex, thousands of identical square windows. Shoulder harness cutting into my neck. *Passive restraint.*

"What a waste," Alan says.

Don't answer. Don't start. Just get home, away from him.

"Maybe I'll join a temple and find an investor there."

"If you pray hard enough."

Wrong tone, too much acid. Now he's looking over at me. Evade him. Just look out the window.

Someone's honking at us. Driver and girlfriend wave Yankee pennants as they pass. We just stare.

Slow, agonizing seconds.

Him: "What?" As in, Go ahead, you might as well get it out.

"Nothing. I just want to get home."

Wringing in the gut.

"If you have something to say, say it."

No point complaining, since there's nothing here I want to salvage. "Forget it. Not worth discussing."

Little exhale from him. "Just what I needed, right after I get my ribs kicked in."

Let him rant all he wants. He knows what he did.

We drive down Second Avenue. Crowd outside a bar celebrating. More honking, but this time it's because Alan cut off a cab.

Silence all the way down to 59th Street. Hairs on my arms bristle when he moves and stirs the air. Then: "You think you have a grievance against me, but that's nothing compared to my grievance against you."

"What? About Suzanne?"

"You know what I mean."

"I was just trying to save your life. I'm sorry you think that's a crime."

"I can't believe your presumption. Deciding what I should and shouldn't know."

"Fine. I'm the world's biggest shit. Great, go ahead and think that."

"How could you keep what she said a secret from me? It's sick!"

"Like I did it to spite you."

Another disgusted breath from him, which pisses me off even more, but neither of us wants to discuss it further, so that's that.

Stuck in my enemy's car, getting a ride home. What could be more pleasant? Clock's green digits glow, colon blinks. Just hold on, in thirty blocks I'll never have to see him again.

6.

LORI HAS POUCHES under her eyes, looks pallid, ill. Walking helps, I think: clean, cool air washes some of the pain away. Better, at least, than sitting in one place and letting it bury her.
"I can't believe I was such a coward. It took a month for me to say something."
"It's a hard thing to do."
Bright yellow leaves on the ground, and some wine-red ones. The path hugs a vertical outcropping of Manhattan schist; can't see a single building.
"He wasn't even trying to hide it any more. He came in late every night and went straight to the shower."
Her face and shoulders twitch.
"If you're cold, you can wear my jacket."
Shakes her head. "He couldn't even look at me."
"What did you say to him, exactly?"
Frowns. "I can't remember."
Unconvincing, but let it go.
I can't tell which way is Fifth Avenue and which way the West Side. I always get lost in this part of the park. Just keep walking, we'll end up somewhere eventually.
"This morning, I wished so hard it was all a dream, for a second I forgot it wasn't."
"What did he say when you brought up the subject?"
"He started crying."
And now *her* face twists up, prologue to tears.
White sky above. A muzzled German shepherd sniffs the path, tugging a woman in a trenchcoat. I can't say, *It'll be all right*, because it won't.
A star-shaped leaf drifts down, deep blotched red, as if someone scraped away the green to expose the blood below. She says, "You know how sometimes you wish you could take back something you said, just erase it?"
"Uh-huh. What did you say?"

"I don't think I want to tell you."
"You don't have to. Only if you want to."
"He was putting his clothes in his suitcase. I went in and asked..."
Don't prod her.
"I asked why he wasn't satisfied with me." Our shoes loud on the pebbles and damp leaves. "It sounds so pathetic."
She's right, it does—in exactly the same way that I was pathetic when I invited Suzanne to sleep with me. We both have known humiliation.
"Did he answer you?"
"He kept saying the last thing in the world he wanted was to hurt me, ever. He said this had nothing to do with me. The sad thing is, I'm so desperate, there have been split-seconds when I let myself believe him."
Unnecessary to ask how she coped after his exit. Assume she cried.
"Did you sleep at all?"
"Yes. I took something, around three o'clock."
I didn't think she had this much candor in her.
A little bird, all black and white streaks, flits around on a thick tree-trunk. I point and she follows my finger. A relief to watch something outside ourselves, something small and interesting and involved in its own business.
"I wish I were a tree," she says, "and didn't have to think."
"Hm."
"It's so foolish to build your whole life around one person. Such a mistake."
Careful here, don't overdo my little speech, don't embarrass her. "Lori? I know I can't make everything right again, but I just want you to know, any time you feel lonely or depressed you can call me and I'll come right over. Any time—you don't have to wait a polite number of days in between. Okay?"
A light breeze, and golden elm leaves rain down behind her. Her eyes so tired, but the dark irises so warm. Grateful.

If only I knew how to take the pain away.

•

"I'm worried about money," she says, looking not at the broad, glittering river below, but at the thumbnail from which she has just chewed a sliver. "I'm not sure I can support myself. I never have, really."
"I thought you made a lot from your children's books."
"Not exactly a lot. Not enough to live on."
"Well, you could try selling your paintings."
She peers down at the Hudson, which is army green today. Though she didn't like that last suggestion, it's a relief to see her wrestling with practical matters instead of wallowing in misery over Alan.
Soaring above us, the great steel X's of the bridge tower. Rocky cliffs of the Palisades, trees touched with orange and yellow. Spectacular place: but not quite spectacular enough to distract her from her troubles.
"I have such mixed feelings," she says. "One minute all I want is for him to come back, and then I remember what happened and I know I couldn't take him back, even if he wanted to come home, because I could never trust him. That's what's so hard. If there were a chance, something to hope for, I could hold onto that, but there isn't."
She looks away from the noisy speedboat below, tiny comet with white tail, and back at her thumb. A lesson for me: a single finger can block out an entire river when it's right in front of your eye.
Two trucks go by, the walkway shakes. I would throw myself over the railing if I thought it would make her notice me, but she'd only go back to brooding about Alan ten minutes later.

•

"What would make you happy?" she asks.
Slouching with the phone at my ear, I share a raised eye-

brow with my reflection in the dark windowpane. No room for candor here, however. "Being a savior."

"That's practical."

"Really. Something like counseling mentally ill people on the street. The problem is, I don't have any idea how to help a crazy person, and also they scare me."

"What about music? You were so happy when you played in the bar."

Painful reminder: I allowed myself euphoria while she suffered. "Somehow I can't believe in that as a career."

"You should, if that's what you really want."

She gives me time to consider her advice. Good opportunity to fantasize. What if she's speaking in code? *If you really want something, you can have it. If you really want me, you can have me.*

"The problem is, I won't be satisfied unless there's an element of social usefulness. Like working as a family doctor in a run-down neighborhood—someplace that can't attract good people because you can't get rich there."

"That sounds perfect for you."

"Except that I can't start pre-med classes at this age."

"Of course you can."

She may be right, but she's also wrong. I don't have it in me. Unless, that is, she married me. Then I could do it with ease.

"Well, you've given me enough food for thought to give me mental heartburn all night. What's new with you?"

"A realtor came over this afternoon to help me set a price for the house."

Crash of illusions hitting the floor. She's fleeing everything to do with Alan; I haven't made a dent. "I didn't know you wanted to sell it."

"I have a hard time being alone here."

She may be unhappy enough to leave New York altogether. And nothing I can say will change that.

"Where would you go, do you think?"

"I'll look for a studio apartment somewhere. Maybe in

your neighborhood. We could go to a coffee shop on weekends for breakfast."

From cautious optimism to despair to radiant hope, in less than thirty seconds. No roller coaster ever went this fast.

"Sounds good to me."

•

Dipping our crispy noodles in duck sauce, cozy and warm in this divey basement restaurant after our frigid walk from the movie theater. Two quick-fingered cooks in white making wontons at the corner table. Proud of myself for leading her on this and our other outings, each better than the one before. The carillon concert, twenty-two stories above Riverside Drive, the carillonneur pounding the keyboard of wooden rods with the bottoms of his fists, the tintinnabulation of the bells, bells, bells, lined up in rows like choirboys, smallest to tallest, clappers the size of baseballs, painful to the ears, especially on the high notes, but Lori grinning, because deafening sound always helps the wounded heart. Our art lesson on the benches by the East River, drawing each others' faces, slowly following the contours of her nose, mouth, jaw, "Don't look at the paper," she said, "keep looking at me," and so I discovered the pattern of veins just visible under the skin of her forehead, and then the Brooklyn Bridge lights came on behind her like a thousand good ideas. And the musical instrument collection at the Metropolitan, the lyre made of a gourd and antelope horns, black swirling spirals, and the speck of soot on her cheek that I wanted to wipe away, an excuse to touch her, and finally did, and she closed her eyes and let me. And the accordions, two dozen of them in Washington Square, playing "Rock Around the Clock" in the cold—short strands of her hair blown back from her forehead, warm breath on my ear when she said, "Did you know my brothers taught me to play 'Viva Las Vegas' on the accordion?" And tonight, the cheap Chinese action movie, when the Hong Kong gangster blew up his rival's yacht and then went to his little boy's birthday party, her whispering, "This is fun!" The pleasure of crudity, without redeeming social value.

And now: waiter brings our hot and sour soup, I'm starved, she tastes the soup and adds some vinegar from the square glass decanter, making it more sour. How graceful and thin her hand is as it tips the decanter. My longing for that hand, and for her white-sleeved arm. Sweet face, a face I should kiss soon, before the opportunity is lost. By the end of tonight?

"I think of Chinese culture as reserved and dignified," she says. "Where did all those gangsters come from?"

"Probably the director met some American businessmen in Hong Kong."

Ponders her brown soup. Lifts a spoonful just above the surface—scratched metal tablespoon, not like the porcelain shovels they give you uptown—and spills it gently back.

"When Wang visited his mistress, I started thinking about my marriage. I know you'll try to reassure me, but I wonder now if he ever loved me. Maybe he just wanted someone safe and unthreatening after she ran out on him. You have to admit, it's hard to see how he could love both her and me."

Although I've always sort of believed exactly what she's saying, hearing her say it shows me that she's wrong. Impatiently, "If he didn't love you, he wouldn't have stolen you from me." (Because he *had* to know I wanted her, people sense these things, it's a lie to pretend otherwise.)

Surprised look, square in my face: noticing me. Thinking-lines between her eyebrows.

Hold her gaze. Let her respond.

She looks down at her soup, dips in and spills out. Seeking words.

Here comes the waiter again, with our entrees, fifteen minutes sooner than expected. "Thanks," she tells him. And to me, "I like this place."

That's the end of that.

Hardly any students around Columbia today, they must be snug in their dorm rooms, studying, philosophizing, making out. A week apart from Lori makes me simply fond of her—no demands, just glad to have her company. Who says I have to push for more?

"I had a dream this morning," I tell her, "where dead people came home once a week for a family dinner, but you had to keep your voice down and treat them very tenderly, or they would leave and never come back."

Sympathetic Lori look, cheeks blushing from the cold. She knows: that the dead visitor was my father, and that the dream was more mournful than I'm admitting.

"You could make it a painting," I say, because her sympathy always makes me uncomfortable. "'Return of the Dead for Sunday Dinner.'"

"That's not a bad idea. The guest could be translucent."

"With the family all watching him solicitously."

"You would have to co-sign it, of course."

Wonder if she ever had this kind of conversation with Alan: reaching for new ideas, seeing them appreciated, then developing them further.

Can't imagine it.

She threads her arm through the angle of my elbow, walks snuggled against me. Unsure what this means—friendship or more? Whatever it is, keep hands in pockets, do nothing to scare her away.

"You must miss your father a lot," she says.

"Yes and no. I think about him every day, but I don't know what to do with it."

"If one of my parents died, I don't know how I would survive."

"What happens is, you don't have a choice. You're just handed this new fact."

Misty drizzle. Open the little umbrella. That's better, now we have a reason to stay close.

Just outside the Broadway gate, a long-bearded street

vendor sticks a green plastic frog on the brick wall. The frog climbs three feet and falls back to the sidewalk, then waddles back to the wall and up again. "Sisyphus the Wonder Frog, one dollar for Sisyphus the Wonder Frog, the frog that takes a fall and keeps climbing the wall."

"I'll take one," say I, playing rube to his huckster. Having Lori on my arm makes me want to spend money, be large-spirited, take part in all things festive.

As we head down Broadway, though, examining the imperfectly molded suction cups on the ugly frog's feet, I can't understand why I bought it.

She shifts so that our linked arms fit more comfortably. "Remember when you asked why I don't show my paintings?"

"Yes."

"I've been turning the question over in my mind since then. I think the real reason is that I hate people assuming they can read my subconscious in my paintings."

Opportunity to make an important point, and also to establish some dignity, as opposed to fawning infatuation. "You just don't want anyone to know what's going on inside you. You're the most private person I know."

"And that's bad?"

"Just frustrating sometimes."

I can feel her going stiff, from shoulders to knees.

"In college, people used to criticize me all the time about this. I still don't understand why a person isn't allowed to be private. Does every single human being on earth have to announce every thought in their head?"

Now she's mad at me—yet we're still walking with arms linked. Each with one shoulder damp from rain.

"Maybe you're right," I say. "I never thought about it that way."

"No, I'm not right, but I don't think I'll ever change."

"Would it help if I just accepted you as you are?"

"No—I don't want to go through life frustrating the people closest to me."

99

Oh. I see. This is about Alan, not me. At least she had the consideration not to speak his name.

Guy and girl kissing on the street, letting the rain wet them. Youthful, rosy faces, standing straight and tall. While our souls writhe.

"Can I tell you something?" she says.

"What?"

"I appreciate your spending so much time with me."

"It's not charity. I need company too."

Dumb reflex, to bat away the exact words I've wanted to hear. Give me another chance and I promise to do better.

"Sometimes I feel hopeless when I'm alone. But you always cheer me up."

"Take the umbrella for a second."

She does, waiting to see why. I put one arm behind her back, one behind her knees, and up she goes, lifted to the sky, or at least as high as my chest.

She smiles with closed lips and holds the umbrella above our heads, but doesn't laugh or put her free arm around my neck, or anything else to tell me *Yes*.

Set her down on the wet gray sidewalk. Cover up. "I just wanted to lift your spirits."

"I see."

Take back the umbrella.

Call me Icarus.

•

Whether because I'm male or because I'm heterosexual, Patty has limited sympathy for my plight. She keeps making an exasperated hissing sound, despite which I keep explaining, pleading my case. "It's not all in my mind. She took my arm and snuggled against me. She looks into my eyes with so much sympathy—but then she turns off. I don't want to be a vulture, picking at her before she's ready, but I really think we could be happy together, and I'm afraid I'll lose my chance if I don't do anything. This is so confusing: I don't know if not kissing her makes me a coward, or if I'm a shit to even want to."

"How would you lose your chance by waiting? I don't understand the logic." Schoolmarmish behind the little round glasses, same height as me but gives the impression of peering down. Make her see. "There's an electricity between us, but it can't last forever. If I wait a year, it'll burn out and die."

"If you were talking about a purely sexual attraction, that might ring true, but I assume you mean more."

Consider that. Is she right?

And while I consider, she plunges ahead. "How can you expect her to get over him so fast? You sound like you want some kind of green light from her, but she can't possibly give it yet, so you get worried and frantic. She was married for seven years, you said—good grief, let her catch her breath."

Hadn't looked at it that way. Patty must think I'm a twit.

We've reached the gate of Columbia, a block above where I lifted Lori four days ago. Funny that Patty and I chose this of all possible lunch-hour routes. Unless I steered us back to the scene of the crime.

"I didn't tell you the whole story. There was also an Embarrassing Moment."

"Uh-oh."

"We felt so close—or, I did. So I picked her up in my arms."

"Go on, yes, what did she do?"

"Nothing. As in, 'I wish you hadn't done that.'"

"And then you wanted to crawl under a rock."

"I'm just worried that now she knows everything I'm thinking, and she'll stay away from me. Unless . . . do you think there's a chance she *doesn't* know what I'm thinking?"

"Who knows? People have an infinite capacity for blindness when it comes to other people being attracted to them. But even if she knows, that's not fatal. She's probably flattered."

"Great. 'I couldn't possibly go out with you, but I'm so flattered.'"

"There's no reason to be gloomy. You may have a chance. You just have to get over your impatience. Give her time to get used to the idea. Stop pushing her."

With that unexpected encouragement, a bright future unfolds before me. Lori kisses me, to signal she's ready. Sex—love—marriage—babies. No reason to doubt, because Patty is wise, Patty is always right.

•

She's late, only ten minutes till the performance, but here she comes, my lovely bride-to-be, hurrying down dark Houston Street with a face full of apology, "I'm so sorry, the train just sat in the tunnel."

Go to her, for the embrace I earned by today's decisive action. "Guess what I did this afternoon?"

She stops short, keeps a space between us that's longer than arms' length—killing my premature hopes and my new career with one blow.

"Hi. What did you do this afternoon?"

Speaking skull: "I registered for biology and inorganic chemistry at NYU. So I can apply to medical school."

"That's great!"

Yeah, whoopee. Don't even *want* to go to medical school now—but must answer her questions, how I'll need two years of courses before applying, etc. I can hear my voice out at the surface of me, while inside, my collapsed spirit analyzes my mistake: I thought I could win her love by proving myself worthy, like the hero who slays the dragon/lion/many-headed monster in order to win the princess. But the king never gives up his daughter willingly; there's always another labor. It doesn't matter what feats I perform, Lori will never be my wife. (Unless I kill the king. Who in this case would be Alan, or her memory of him. A more formidable adversary than any monster.)

Down the steps and into the small smoky room. "What's wrong?" she asks. "You look so sad."

Can't believe she really doesn't know. "Nothing. Let's just have drinks and get drunk."

And so we do, or at least one drink apiece. Just enough to feed the bitter grouse in me who wouldn't mind if he never saw another one of these mediocre performance pieces. She asks how long before I'll actually be a doctor, and my stomach sours as I tick off the years of school, internship, residency. Without her, I doubt I'll even show up on the first day of classes.

First act: Two guys pantomiming a dull married couple, one dabbing imaginary furniture with a pink feather duster and striking provocative poses that go unnoticed by the other, who's rehearsing a speech, hammering palm with fist and pausing meaningfully. Weighty sighs from the duster, ignored by the orator. Okay, okay, we get the idea, a decayed TVish marriage, nothing new here. Why does everyone assume they'll do better than their parents, anyway? But then, golden light pours over the two, startling them both into attention. Percussive synthesizer music; their mouths open in awe. Each reaches curiously into the other's round gape (*there's* something you don't see every day) and pulls out a streamer, one purple, one green. They back away from each other, and the streamers keep coming, ten feet, twenty feet. The light changes colors, the men draw snaking waves with the streamers, dancing in an ecstatic Carnival-in-Rio sort of stomp. When the light and music abruptly stop, leaving us in the dark with the squeaking of their sneakers as they hurry offstage, the audience shouts, claps, whistles. Even in my sulk, I can't deny that it was good.

Lights on. At all the tables around us, smiles of aesthetic pleasure. Two waitresses in cut-offs and tank tops hustle to take drink orders.

"I've never seen anything like that," says Lori.

"I don't know what it meant, but it made everyone so happy."

A moment later, though, a zig-zag chain of thought leads me to understanding: 1) I will never experience the kind of ecstasy they portrayed. 2) Unless, that is, I tell Lori everything I've been thinking and she says, *I feel the same way.* 3) That's the greatest pleasure in the world, prying the truth from each other and discovering mutual love.

"Those streamers were so original," she says. "I never thought of doing that, inventing images that go so far beyond ordinary surrealism."

"Lori. I want to talk to you."

Quiets down to let me speak, so swiftly that I wonder if she has been expecting this for weeks. Closed mouth: maybe calm, or maybe clenching her teeth. Thirty seconds from now, she will either be in my arms or out of reach forever.

"There's a reason why I looked depressed before. It's about you." Steady gaze from her, more compassion than distress. "I know this is premature, but I can't stop thinking about you. When I went to hug you before, and you stepped back . . . I understand, you're still getting over what happened, but I've wanted so much to touch you. Don't worry, I can control myself. I just had to explain."

Hint of her enigma smile. Can't tell what she's going to say, which way this will go.

"You're so honest. And brave."

Praise to soften the blow. "Thanks. Now it's your turn."

"I'll try," while behind her a waitress on tip-toes reaches over the bar, how odd that I'm staring at another woman's behind while my beloved deals me my fate. "I knew you were attracted to me. I'm attracted to you too. I admire how much you care about doing something worthwhile with your life. And I appreciate how gentle and generous you've been with me. I've even imagined forgetting everything and going out with you, just being happy. But I'm so confused right now—you don't know how confused I am. The truth is, I don't want to risk losing you. I need you too much."

Big band music comes from the speakers, and the two waitresses take a break to jitterbug together, sweating and laughing. *I'm attracted to you too. I admire you.* Exhilaration that cancels out everything else.

"But," she says, "I know I don't have the right to monopolize your time when I don't know when or if I'll ever be ready to go out with you."

Don't want to leave paradise yet. "Were you attracted when we first met? Did I make the mistake of my life by not kissing you that time when you sat on my lap?"

"It was different then. I would have gone out with you, but I wouldn't have appreciated you the same way."

I would have gone out with you. Fool, fool, fool. You delay, you examine twelve sides of every issue, you squander every chance. "I wish I'd realized."

"So what should we do now?" she asks.

"Well. Maybe we could keep spending time together. I'll just have to adjust my thinking. No expectations, at least for the immediate future."

"That would make me so happy. Are you really willing to do that?"

"It's better than not seeing you at all."

All four of our hands resting on the metal rim of this pizza-sized table. Too bad I can't touch her.

"You're noble," she says.

"No. Bull."

The lights dim, a relief. Maybe I can touch her, just a little. Hold her hand, that's acceptable after what we just said.

She accepts, by squeezing. Go further: stroke the back of her hand with the back of mine. Not too lightly, though, don't be erotic.

And WHAM, here she is, banging against my shoulder. A reprimand? No, snuggling.

Don't think, don't worry. Kiss the top of her head, where the hair is so thin. Frail Lori, so shy and tense.

Turning her face up to me, to be kissed—and then opening her lips, touching my tongue with the tip of hers.

(Maybe tonight. Despite everything she said.)

A spotlight shines on a woman wearing a bonsai tree as a hat. Lori straightens up as if the spotlight had fallen on

her. The performer, immobile, says, "I didn't bring this on myself. A man did it to me. He thought he was a god."
Lori's hand disengages and slips away.
Nevertheless, a night of miracles.

•

I can smell my own sweat, and it's not a good smell: the sweat of loading her suitcases, art supplies and easel into her father's van, *Feig Meats,* and then unloading them here, in this Long Island split-level with the mildew smell in the bathroom, the place she came from but grew out of years ago. Yet here she is, slicing her brisket, calm as Buddha while her mother hides her sorrow and asks me how it is that some people don't learn to read.

"It usually isn't a matter of not having the opportunity," I explain, every bit as miserable as Mrs. Feig and dissembling just as much. "Most of the students have some kind of learning problem."

No need to fear that her mother will ask me to elaborate, because she barely heard me. Like her husband, she's intent on Lori, and grief-stricken. While Lori, who should be miserable, chews blankly in her valium trance.

"You really want to sell the house?" Mr. Feig blurts.

Lori finishes chewing, swallows, and says, "The realtor is showing it tonight."

"What's the hurry?" Mrs. Feig asks. "You can sell it later, you don't have to decide so fast."

Amiably, without acknowledging conflict, "I've already decided."

On the wall behind her parents, above their heads, a cheery sunburst clock from the era of Doris Day movies. Within the next hour or so, I'll get on a train by myself and that will be the end of what never began.

I have to talk to her, but she's not here, she left a cardboard Lori to take her place.

"Did you know," she tells me, "that my father was a violinist?"

Shakes his head, refusing the compliment, too busy mourning.

"He didn't want to work in his father's butcher shop because his father had lost a finger."

"Did you actually work as a musician?" I ask him.

"Not often enough to feed a family," his wife answers sourly.

Hard to recognize in her the efficient, wisecracking homemaker who wouldn't let me help clear the table the last time I came, who said, "Sit down or I'll shoot."

We cut our meat in silence, until Mrs. Feig abruptly pushes her chair out and disappears into the kitchen. Sound of her knocking jars around the refrigerator to reach something in back, maybe dessert, or else a heartburn remedy.

I have an ambition. I want to make all of them happy again. I want to come back to this house a year from now as Lori's partner, both of us radiant, and burn away the memory of this day.

Creak of footsteps in the kitchen above, muffled by the acoustic ceiling tile. Harold and me at his pool table, Harold chalking his cue. Interesting man: kindly butcher, shy musician, owner of a pool table. Plus, the way he turned his head away to hide his emotion as he helped unload the van. I assume he wants to ask what's going on with his daughter, how can he help her, but so far he hasn't said a word.

"Go ahead and break," he says, so I do, harder than is polite. My own frustrations leaking out.

Studying the balls, "You're a close friend of Alan's, right?"

Uh-oh. "Uh-huh."

"Does he know what the hell he's doing?"

Buy time. "In what way do you mean?"

"Is he really going through with this, or will he get over it and come back?"

"I can't tell you. I don't know."

He sinks three balls in a row—strange that he's bothering with the game, now that we've gotten to the point—and

narrowly misses his fourth shot. Nods to me to go. Orange-striped ball drops into the pocket, but so does the cue ball. Leaning on his cue as if it were a shepherd's staff, he twists until his back makes an audible crack. His turn, but he's not shooting. "I don't understand him. He always looked happy with her."
"It surprised me too."
Studies the possible shots. "You can give him a message when you see him."
Butcher, knives, balls. Watch out.
"Tell him he owes me money."
He drives the red ball hard into the side pocket. I have two choices here. Could say nothing, and get revenge, or protect Alan. He deserves punishment. However...
"I think, before you do anything, you should know that he had a lot of problems with this woman in college. It was very stormy, he never got over it completely. Now it's like a compulsion, something he has to finish and be done with."
"You don't think it'll last?"
"I don't know. Just, I would wait before doing anything final."
Another shot, and the eight ball drops loudly into the corner pocket. For a shy violinist, he's pretty furious. "Let's hope you're right."
Right. Let's hope Alan comes back to Lori. Yep.

Mrs. Feig alone at the kitchen table, coffee and cigarette, one side of her face pushed up by the hand she's leaning on. Weary past smiling.
"Time for me to head home."
"Okay. She's in her room."
If the pill has worn off, maybe we can say a real goodbye. Although face it, nothing good can happen, since half the motive for her move is that she can't deal with me.
On her knees next to her childhood bed, neither crying nor praying, but reaching under the scalloped dust ruffle. Her parents have preserved this room as scrupulously as if it were a national historic site. Not a wrinkle in the stars-

and-snowflakes bedspread, not a knickknack out of place on the desk. Frosted-glass perfume bottle, purple troll, tiny gold-framed "Blueboy" on a tiny gold easel: absolute ordinariness, Lori before she became Lori.

Out from under the bed come two stiffened watercolors. "I did these in high school. In a way, I like them better than anything I've done since."

The two paintings show this house, one in fall, one in winter. The white paper is the snow.

"They're pretty."

"I think I'll frame them and put them over the desk."

On the dresser, three pictures of her. Little girl reaching up to a doorknob; adolescent with braces and a violet dress; and high school graduate with great warm eyes, glossy hair, familiar tight smile. I long for the impossible, to have known her all those years, to be the man who was always there, unnoticed, until the film cleared from her eyes and she recognized her true love.

"Lori. I have to go now."

Sitting on her heels at bedside, not looking at me. "You were nice to help."

"I'm going to miss you," I say. *Snap out of it. Turn and face me.*

"Don't miss me. Come visit."

Last chance. "It's sad to me that you're so far away. I got used to spending time with you."

"I'm not gone forever. I'll come over for dinner some Sunday."

Smiling at some private joke. I may be selfish to want so much, and foolish to have thought I could get it, but I'm also angry enough at her coolness to leave without another word. Though if she touched me I would forgive everything.

Rest a hand on her sweatered shoulder.

She puts hers on top of mine: ice.

"Get home safe."

"If you say so."

A shame. To adore someone, and to have no choice but to pour your unwanted love down the drain.

7.

THE GUITAR, BALANCED across my belly, teeters each time I breathe in. No energy for playing, or for putting the dinner dishes in the sink, or for getting out of bed.

If a drug could make her feel no emotion, then couldn't an opposite drug make her feel more? Call a pharmaceutical company—-perhaps such a thing already exists. Or change course, from med school to neuroscience, and search for the wrinkle of the brain that, when stimulated, yields love.

Thuck-bong, my defective doorbell. Police? Or else *her:* one day apart was all it took, she's come back to me.

Check my hair in the glass of the Nicaraguan literacy poster, there I am next to Sandino. "Who is it?"

Three sung notes, "Su-za-anne," simultaneous with the sight of her through the peephole lens, lush and convex.

What now?

Broad olive face, eyes so full of intelligence that you have to brace yourself to not get blown over. So much of her: wild black hair spread across her shoulders, infinite coils.

She purrs: "We're still friends, right?"

"Sure. Come on in."

Kiss, soft lips. Surveying—long time since she was here last. Guitar on unmade bed, abandoned plate of spaghetti, *Voice* opened to the capsule movie reviews. Must look so impoverished to her, Burt's little box.

She sits in the easy chair, sandals resting on the couch. Denim jacket with the rose on the back, and that baby-powder scent. Snug black jeans, big smile. "Congratulations. You've just won a fun-filled trip to the Island of Coney, complete with your own date to ride the roller coaster with."

What's that supposed to mean? Clear the table while I probe her intentions. "Coney Island is a long subway ride away."

"You sound so old. Come on, we have a car."

Aha. *We.* "Alan's car? With Alan in it?"

"Stop cleaning. He knows he hurt your feelings, he wants to apologize. You don't know how much pressure he's been under."

Odd to hear her speak without irony. Doesn't quite sound like her; a buzz in her voice.

"Sit, Burt. Down."

Instead of facing her on the couch, I sit at the table, where we can talk sidewise. "I think we'd better let dead dogs lie."

She swings over to the couch, legs along its length, so she can look me square in the face. "I shouldn't tell you this, but it's the only way you'll understand. He lied on a loan application, he exaggerated how much rent he takes in, and now it looks like the bank may have caught him, and it's a federal offense—literally. That's why he acted the way he did: he's a nervous wreck, he thinks they're going to put him in prison."

None of which he mentioned to me, his bosom buddy.

"I'm sorry, but I don't see how dragging out a used-up friendship will help him."

"You *can't* lose each other because of one night."

"This isn't because of one night. I've been putting up with subtle slights for ten years."

"You think he doesn't respect you enough?"

That she sees proves it's true. "Something like that."

Shaking her head, "That's just your personal dread. Alan thinks you're the greatest guy in the world."

"You don't—"

Stop. Can't justify myself without going into the humiliating specifics.

"Come on, he's waiting downstairs. With your date."

What is she talking about? On the other hand, it doesn't matter. "Suzanne, I really don't want to see him."

"You're going to abandon him when he needs you?"

Hold tight. Defend with silence. Don't yield.

"You don't know how miserable he is about what happened. He loves you."

Evade her, look down. At the hardening loops of spaghetti, and the Belgian documentary I circled, about a man born without legs or arms.

"Coney Island, Burt. A return to the simple fun of yesteryear. Remember?"

She means the night Alan ate twelve varieties of junk food and had to lie on the sidewalk after riding the Cyclone. Mischievous grin, certain I'll give in, because how could I resist her?

"I don't know if I can look him in the face."

She comes around behind me, puts her hands on my shoulders. "Don't worry. It's dark out."

•

Yes, but he's double-parked beneath a streetlight, and there, through the windshield, is his face. Spasm in my jaw; how long have I been clenching my teeth?

"B-man!"

Climb into the back and find the Russian girl from Suzanne's office, the teenager. Alan twists in his seat to shake hands, I have no choice but to accept, the penalty for yielding to Suzanne. He gives my hand a meaningful squeeze, as if we're best friends again, which pumps rage into my throat. Not sure how long I can keep from exploding.

"Burt, remember Rima?"

Black bomber jacket, close-cropped platinum hair, an ugly hardness in the shape of her mouth. Smell of liquor, too.

"Hi."

A nod from her, or else just a twitch.

Cold in the car, because Alan has his window open. As if reading my angry mind, he explains: "A squirrel or something must have climbed into the motor and died, the car has an odor. I searched with a flashlight but couldn't find anything. I'll push the heat up."

There it is: a smell like rotting garbage.

"Pretend we're going to the beach," says Suzanne, and turns on the radio, loud. Something heavy-metalish, too new for me to know. She swings her feet out the open passenger window and sings over the radio, "Surf City, here we come!" Alan won't pull out, though, until she brings her feet back inside.

How oppressive and annoying all this vivacity is.

Alan addresses the guest in the mirror. "Rima, have you ever been to Coney Island?" Making her welcome, showing what a nice guy he is.

"Yes. I live in next town."

Thick, stereotypical accent, down to the left-out *the*. If I didn't know she worked with Suzanne, I'd assume she was putting it on.

"This is like a reunion for us, Rima," Suzanne says. "We went to Coney Island once when we were in college. We ate cotton candy and rode the Cyclone, the old roller coaster."

"Does anyone know if the rides are open this time of year?" I ask the front seat in general.

"Even if some things are closed," Suzanne says, "the arcades stay open all winter. And the bumper cars are indoors."

Over to West Street. Lightless factories along the river, less ugly by night than by day.

Alan adjusts the mirror to find my eyes. "Do you remember what we talked about in the car the last time we went to Coney Island?"

Ten years ago, how would I? "No."

"Our future life stories? My baby food company?"

"Right!" Suzanne says. "Burt made yours up—about you climbing the corporate ladder, and finding out they were thinning their infant formula with flour, and your conscience made you blow the whistle."

Was that Coney Island night? I've separated the two in my memory.

"They tried to discredit me by calling me insane, and I ended up punching out the CEO at a press conference. But Suzanne had a million dollars from the lottery, so she lent me enough to build my own baby food business, and then the government sued my old company and they went bankrupt, leaving me as the world's third largest manufacturer of baby foods."

"Hm."

"I can't remember much of mine," Suzanne says. "I had a job in the embassy in Moscow, and Alan came to live with me, and we got arrested for something. But what happened in the end?"

None of us remembers, not even Alan, who made it up.

"The Woman Who Forgot her Future," she says.

"What was your story?" Alan asks me.

"I went to Africa with the Peace Corps."

"Right, and fell in love with a village girl. What happened then?"

"She came back to New York with me."

"Yes! You had to rescue her family from a famine and a flood, so they all came to live in your apartment."

"With a baby elephant," Suzanne chimes in. "And then the landlord evicted you because the lease said no pets, so you all went to live in Central Park."

Alan laughing, tears in his eyes, determined to make this a merry night. There was more to the story (a bum I used to give quarters to left me a shopping bag full of money, I bought an apartment building, converted it into a homeless shelter) but I have no desire to fill in the gaps, because Suzanne's story humiliated me. Here was the sexiest woman I knew, calling me a bleeding-heart chump. Afraid of confirming the stereotype, I changed my mind about joining the Peace Corps after college, and wondered forevermore what it would have been like.

The highway lights glint from her eyes as we enter the Brooklyn-Battery Tunnel. Point of no return: too late to say, *Stop the car* and climb out.

Exhaust mingles with Suzanne's perfume and Rima's

stale cigarette smell. Red taillights ahead become flickering flames on the endless tiles of the white tunnel wall. Note the ring of pale skin on Alan's finger, where the gold band used to be. Suzanne twirling his hair with a fingertip, trying to make it corkscrew the way it did in college, but the hair isn't long enough. Alan's right hand seeking warmth between her thighs. Constant touch, like long ago. He always gets what he wants.

Around the rim of Brooklyn, past the immense Verrazano Bridge, until we can see the old parachute jump in the distance, a black skeleton against the evening sky. Ordinarily, this is a beloved sight, Brooklyn's Eiffel Tower, a piece of our parents' Coney Island, but tonight it means nothing to me.

Off the highway, down dull Ocean Parkway to the end, Surf Avenue—where all the rides are dark. Astro-Land locked, security guy eating a hero behind the fence. Not a light to be seen on the Wonder Wheel. Even the bumper cars are out of sight behind gray gates. Solitary black men leaning against buildings. The carnival has closed for the winter.

What's left? Nathan's Famous, *Open All Year,* multicolored neon. One customer at the counter, light spilling onto the empty sidewalk, Edward Hopper does fast food. Also, the blinking yellow bulbs of the Faber's Fascination sign, video games loud enough to hear from the moving car.

Suzanne staring out her window. Quietly, "Anyone for a dip in the ocean?"

Alan won't give up. "We can go to Nathan's, then see what new video games they have in the arcade."

"How's that with you two?" Suzanne asks us.

"Hot dog," say I.

"Is okay," Rima shrugs.

Stillwell Avenue, in the summer you can't find a space here but tonight only one other car's parked. Three of us huddle separately in the cold while Alan sets up the Club on the steering wheel. Protecting the last of his possessions.

Ten years ago, Nathan's seemed a slice of history, relic

of a WWII movie with skinny Frank Sinatra. Tonight it's just shabby, and no great bargain either, $1.79 for a frank, $1.59 for the ripple-cut French fries. Alan to Suzanne, a worried mumble, "Is there anything you can eat?"

Whoops, her stomach, no fats or oils. An all-out fiasco.

"I'll take my chances with the clams," she says.

"We don't have to stay, we could go somewhere else."

"Don't. It's not worth making a fuss over."

Though he pays for Suzanne and Rima, Alan has sense enough not to try to pay for me. Each of us carries his or her tray to the chest-high steel table. They must have designed this place to be cleaned with a hose, down to the center-drained tile floor. Is this what morgues look like?

Alan asks Rima how her hot dog compares to Russian food, and she says, "I like Pinna Colada Bang. Rest is shit."

When we're down to the butts of our franks, Suzanne tells Rima something in Russian and leads her out to the sidewalk. Points to the D train parked on the elevated tracks across the intersection, last stop, and tells some laughing tale.

"I can't blame you for being mad at me," Alan says, unexpectedly direct. "I know I acted like a jerk. I just want you to know, there's no one else whose friendship matters more to me."

A soulful gaze, and my innards start to melt. He's sincere, he's contrite. Who could resist such an open heart?

But forgiveness must be delayed—for dignity's sake, and because one moist-eyed look doesn't erase that treacherous *sssss* at the ballpark.

"I've been so messed up over my business problems. Not that that excuses anything."

"Did you find an investor?"

"I've been reconsidering my goals. I may sell everything and start a different business, something that would give me more freedom of movement."

No mention of the possible indictment. A minor omission.

"So things are good with Suzanne?"

"Absolutely great."

"What about Lori? What are you planning to do?"

Solemn frown. "I talked to a lawyer. We have to do a separation agreement. After a year, that converts automatically to a divorce. But every time I think about calling her, I remember the night I moved out and I can't pick up the phone."

"Why? What do you mean?"

"She didn't want me to see her cry. I hurt her, and she never deserved to get hurt."

With one thumb, he mashes what's left of his hot dog bun into a pancake. Remorse.

"You have to call her," I say. "Leaving her hanging isn't a kindness. She may think you're coming back."

Rolling the bun-dough into a pellet, "Have you seen her?"

"I helped her move back to her parents' house yesterday. She's very depressed. You have to let her get on with her life."

Suzanne glances back at us but Alan doesn't see, because his conscience is projecting an image of Lori on the paper plate.

"Her father mentioned the loan. Is that what's stopping you?"

"Not at all. I've already put a building up for sale so I can pay him back."

He looks up at Suzanne, stronger now. Resolved.

And that's the signal for our dates to return, Smile and Pout. "Who wants to try the boardwalk?" he asks, a jarring jump in volume.

"Oh, yippee," Suzanne tweets.

No objections from Rima, nor from me. Alan dumps our paper plates, puts an arm around my shoulder, which I endure, and leads us out.

On the midway, every stall is shuttered. Alan lets go of me, a relief, and goes back to Suzanne. Past a closed corn-dog stand and some hibernating rides, Alan and Suzanne's arms X'ed across each others' backs as in college. A&S,

everyone called them, two people merged into one. He kisses the side of her throat, and she whispers something in his ear. Weird to see them together again, as if the last seven years never happened.

Sloshing to my right. Rima capping a flat half-pint of Jim Beam, slipping it into the pocket of her bomber jacket.

"So, Rima, how much English do you know?"

"Fuck you. Shit and piss."

"Okay. The practical stuff."

She belches.

"And what do you think of America?"

"I have no friends here. Is lonely."

A switching of gears is called for, from self-defense to compassion. Not easy. "How do you spend your time?"

"Listen to music, go to work, get drunk."

She pulls a chewed piece of gum out of her mouth and sticks it on the side of the bottle protruding from her pocket.

"You don't have friends at work?"

Lights a cigarette, says no more. I misunderstood. She's not looking for sympathy—not from me, anyway.

Splopsh, one sneaker lands in a puddle. A snort from her.

Up the wooden ramp, past fecal-stinking dumpster, to the boardwalk. No one in sight up here, except a hooded guy two streetlamps down. Black ocean, icy wind. Our shoulders hunch, hands take refuge in pockets. A ketchup-smeared Nathan's napkin scrapes across the diagonal planking, pushed by wind.

"Last one in is a rotten egg," Suzanne says.

"We'll warm up as we walk, " Alan offers, but Suzanne has stopped walking, she's at the railing, watching the black ocean recede to infinity.

"Look at the moon," Alan says. "What a clear night."

She doesn't look at the moon, doesn't move. Waves break; a sickly paralysis blurs her face.

Rima walks on alone, bored to death, heading toward the blinking red light of the parachute jump. Alan in distress, can't be in two places at once, protecting Rima from the guy in the hood and helping Suzanne through this grim spasm.

"I'll stay here," I say. Though reluctant to leave Suzanne's side, he catches up with Rima as she takes another slug from the bottle.

Now that we're alone, Suzanne walks. What's the word? *Perverse.*

"Will you come to our wedding?" she asks. "It'll be very small. Teeny."

"If you invite me, I'll come."

She's peering down at the planks, or else between them, at the paper cups and crumpled burger wrappers you can see below if you focus beyond the wood. The man in the hooded sweatshirt is trimming his nails with blunt scissors under the streetlamp. No voices reach us, only the loud, dirty ocean.

Alan calls back, "Look at those tankers way out there. See the lights?"

Suzanne, a broken-voiced cry, "What are you so fucking happy about? *Always.*"

We keep walking, all of us. Alan goes back to his conversation with Rima. If we ignore it, the wind will blow it away, as if the words were never spoken.

Remember this about Suzanne: if you get close to her, sooner or later she'll turn and slash you.

"He refuses to admit we have any problems whatsoever," she says. "He could get shot in the face and say everything's peachy."

The obvious question is, *What problems do you have?* Before I can ask, she answers. "He bends every which way to fit me, but I'm so twisted, it's hopeless."

A gust goes through my jacket.

"Unfortunately, he knows I don't admire his life's work, so now he wants to start over, which would be awful because he is what he is, through and through. Tell me if you see a solution, because I don't."

Do I? Ummmm . . . .

"The only comfortable time we have left is when we're asleep: when he holds me all night and we forget everything in the dark."
"Did you mean, before, that you're actually planning a wedding, or was that sarcastic?"
"No, it's real. Rings, relatives, the whole nine hogs."
"But why? If you feel the way you do."
"I promised myself I wouldn't leave him this time, no matter what. I may make us both miserable, but I won't run away."
Miniature smile, her way of grimacing. Up ahead, Rima throwing up over the railing, Alan helpless at her side.
He got what he wanted, now he has to live with it.

•

We're all too cold to keep the windows open this time, so we sit amid the smell of dead animal. Rima rests her bottle on her kneecap, taking comfort from the shape in her hand. Suzanne picks the plastic foam sleeve from an empty Diet Coke bottle, making a thin spiral strip. Fidgety fingers: the sleeve resists at the seam and she attacks it impatiently, nails pecking the glass.

Alan keeps his eyes on the road, both hands on the bottom of the wheel. Quietly enduring, ready for further eruptions.

"Here," Rima says. "Turn here."

Brick bungalow squeezed in among twenty just like it, weedy driveways dividing house from house. Changing blue TV glow on the windowshade, man shouting in Russian, answered in English, "No!"

"Thanks for coming, Rima," says Alan.

"Good night." Quick Russian mumble to Suzanne, scantly returned. Not a word to me.

Without her, the silence thickens. Let's hope they can hold off fighting until I'm gone.

A hinged snake of plastic foam dangles from the bottle into Suzanne's lap. She tears it off and balls it up in one hand. "Wasn't tonight fun?" she turns to ask me. Scary grin.

"Relatively speaking, it was not unfun."

Faces front again. "Commence evasive action, right, Burt?"

Alan: "Suzanne—"

"Yes, dear?"

"What do you want him to say?"

She throws the balled-up plastic at the windshield. It comes to rest in the narrow angle between glass and dash. That's it, outburst's over. Alan checks me in the mirror, assessing the damage. Nothing fatal, just a public naming of my weakness. Not that hard to bear, since unlike him, I don't have to live with this for the rest of my life.

(Memories of college, of giggled mockeries suffered through the years. Used to be, she would hit a nerve and I would conceal the shame with nonchalance, which couldn't have fooled anyone. Lounge of Otsego Hall, Alan dancing on a table, drunk to oblivion, Suzanne annoyed at him. "I have to piss," he laughs. There's a dented pot on the hot plate in the corner, so I bring it over to the table, a joke. "Oh Burt, I think you should hold it up for him," she says. A burning-face moment. How good it is to be older, beyond her reach.)

"Sorry, Burt," she says. "I seem to be out of control tonight."

"That's true, you do."

Playfully, "I promise it'll never happen again."

"See that it doesn't."

False babble, spoken to smooth my exit. In fact, I intend to refuse her company from now on.

There's Alan in the mirror again, apologizing with sad eyes for what's not his fault. In a way, Suzanne succeeded tonight: I've forgiven him completely.

At my building, he turns to say, "We should go to a Knicks game, the season starts next week."

"Sure."

"I'll give you a call."

"Good."
Suzanne facing straight ahead. " 'Night, Burt."
"Yep."
From my doorway, one last glance. Alan checking traffic to his left, then one hand raised to me, no smile, before pulling out. Suzanne with head back, eyes closed.
Good night, A&S. Mercy upon your souls.

8.

A HURRICANE MAY or may not hit the city tonight, a late-season storm that has already torn apart coastal areas in North Carolina and New Jersey. Lori should arrive any minute. If the hurricane strikes, she won't be able to get back to Long Island, will have to stay over, and then . . . if only I could say, Who knows?, but I can't, because tonight holds no good possibilities. Coming out of her skin on the phone, "I can't stay here or I'll go crazy," aftermath of Alan's call, the one I told him to make, the one about divorce.

Lasagna's almost done baking, ordinarily a weapon of seduction but not tonight. Masking-tape asterisks on both windows, as they advised on the news, protection against shattered glass. Put on a cassette (Pan-pipes and charangos from the Andes, no words to distract) and set out the wine and glasses. Not to get her drunk, just to numb some of the pain.

Discreet knock, a one-knuckler. Her first time here alone since she met Alan.

Tears in her eyes, but that may be from the wind, which has also reddened her cheeks. No kiss, only a blurted "It smells delicious!"

She hangs her coat on one of the pegs by the door. Longsleeve T-shirt with inappropriately cheerful stripes, green and blue. "Let's watch the news," she says, "I want to see what the hurricane is doing." Goes to the kitchen and turns on the countertop TV, while I set out the salad and bowls. *"A family of six had a narrow escape today as they huddled for shelter in the bathroom of their New Jersey home, the only room not exposed to the buffeting winds. They listened in terror as windows blew in, walls tore away, and the roof blew off."*

Join her, standing in the shoebox kitchen. Leaves whirl around in the alley as we watch a repeat of last night's videotape, beach-house sinking into the ocean after its pilings fold like a stooping camel's legs. Destruction as distraction; a brief relief.

"We can move the TV into the other room if you'd like." She shuts it, "Sorry, I'm being rude," takes the corkscrew from me and slips out to the living room. Pours wine into the two tumblers. Let's time this: how long can she go without referring to Alan or divorce?

Sipping, she takes in my artifacts. Postcard collection, Sandinista poster, souvenir paperweights from childhood (stegosaurus, mini-bust of Jefferson). Looking everywhere but in my eyes.

"What do you see? Bachelor squalor?"

"No, I like your apartment. It's cozy and efficient."

Closely examines the photo of my parents kissing in front of the Seattle Space Needle, pre-me.

"I never saw them do that in person," I comment.

No response. Her gaze comes to rest on the easy chair facing the couch: threadbare armrests, Mandela T-shirt covering cola-stained back cushion. Where she sat in my lap seven years ago and I didn't have the nerve to kiss her.

"My family used to have that same chair when I was growing up," she says.

I know. We had this conversation the last time.

The windows rattle. Sounds bad outside—increasing chance of overnight complication.

Nasty buzz of alarm clock. Wake up, lasagna's ready.

My small table can barely hold this feast: salad in yellow colander, bowls, wine bottle (already half-gone), liter of Pepsi, four tumblers, two plates of lasagna, salad dressing, utensils. Good thing I forgot to make the garlic bread. "You gave me too much," she says, almost happy. The wondrous power of pasta and red sauce.

Three minutes later, though, while I'm lifting the fork above my head, clowning with a string of mozzarella that won't break, she coughs a mouthful back onto her plate and sobs.

Fork down. Stand behind her, hands on her shaking shoulders. She turns her face against my belly, breath warm through my shirt. Don't speak. Just stroke her hair: weightless strands that catch in my calluses.

Flat on the couch, her knees hooked over the armrest, hasn't cried in a few minutes. "I'm okay," she says, and sits up slowly, puffy-eyed, flushed in the cheeks. Behind her on the windowsill is Sisyphus the Wonder Frog, souvenir of better times.
"I'm sorry about all this."
"Don't worry about it."
Blinking her eyes clear.
"Thanks for putting up with me. Once again." Reaches across the narrow gap and touches my knee. Flinch of twisted desire.
"I'm sorry, I forgot about your accident. Does it still hurt?"
"No, it's numb, and anyway it was the other knee."
Compressed laugh. *Touch me again, Lori.* She stares at my knees while her thoughts wander away from me.
"There's a screw in there somewhere. The carpentry kind. When I saw it on the X-ray, I jumped."
Cold draft from the window behind her. Moaning wind suggests the end of the world—when anything's allowed.
"Remember when we were sitting just like this and you came over and sat in my lap?"
"Yes."
A brown oak leaf flies up between the window-sashes, then rocks gently downward onto her leg. Shadows under her red eyes. I long to comfort her.
So go ahead: cross over to the couch. And here she comes, snuggling in against me. Clean-smelling skin, wine on her breath. A closeness like never before.
"Lori. I still..."
No, I can't say it. But there's another way. Slouch down so we're face to face. Show her what it would be like with me. Touch her lips with mine, infinite tenderness, as if the slightest excess pressure would burst her.
She opens her mouth wide, presses it hard against mine,

clumsy but passionate. Overwhelming—weird, wrong. But this time I will not squander my chance. Squeeze her waist under the loose top, move hands higher. She keeps kissing me, eyes closed, allowing everything.

In the alley, something smashes. She pulls away, turns to the window behind us, sees our quivering reflection. "We should move," I whisper, because if the battering wind breaks the glass, we may get slashed, masking tape or no. She nods, agreeing, but pulls me back into the kiss. Back go my hands under her top.

If this is a mistake—if Lori doesn't know what she's doing, and blames me later—too bad. If Alan never speaks to me again, I accept that too. Unhook the bra. Lift the striped shirt.

She presses my hand, with the cotton hem in it, to her sternum. Stopping me. "I don't know about this," she murmurs.

Soberly, despite exasperation, "What are you thinking?"

"That my motives are wrong, and we'll both end up regretting it."

"Unless tonight begins something permanent."

Rests her chin on our joined hands. "I just don't know if we would work as a couple."

"I have a very clear picture of how it would be. We would get along exactly the way we do now—only better." I.e., because we could lie naked in bed together, which always helps. But I can't say that.

She stands up and straightens her top. "I think we'd better not." Starts clearing the table. My right arm tingles with blood where her back pressed against me. No use arguing.

Solemn cleanup, three trips apiece to the kitchen, elbows bumping in the narrow doorway. Scrape the hardened lasagna off the plates, stack the dishes in the sink. She, out in the living room, wipes the table with the smelly old sponge that I wish I'd replaced.

Finished in the kitchen, I find her curled on her side on my bed, face hidden, in mourning. Stay away, let her be.

(Divorce, end of her marriage. Abandoned, unwanted.)

All right, then, sit on the edge of the bed. Warm hand on her cold ankle. For her sake, not mine.

Bloodshot eyes. "I don't want to feel like this any more."

Go behind her, curl against her back. Hold her around the ribs, press close. She encloses both of my hands in both of hers.

Kiss her neck, the hot unhappiness there.

She turns to face me. Eyes closed, she kisses me again, softly now. Another change of heart.

"Turn the light out, okay?"

To the far end of the room, hit the switch. Floodlight in the alley casts the shadow of the frog up onto the ceiling, a gargoyle. There's Lori, beneath the blue light of the receiver's dial, waiting patiently for me. Music stopped long ago, I didn't notice. Nuzzle under her top, kiss her belly—smell of soap, dampness. Bra still undone. Lift it, first sight of her breasts: small but pretty. Discreet pink nipples.

Undressing, side by side on the edge of the bed, taking off shoes and socks. Impossible to do this gracefully, just get through it.

Her head on my pillow, hands folded on her navel. Must be as strange for her to see my body as it is for me to see hers, after all these years. Unexpected birthmarks and hairs.

Hold her against me, so warm. Nothing between us, not even air. Slide a hand down below, but she intercepts it. "Lie on top of me?"

Give her what she wants: to be covered, anchored, held. So comfortable, as if our bodies were made to fit together, like lock and key. Sense that it can't get better than this, that maybe we should stop here and preserve this closeness.

Too bad that's impossible.

She watches my fingers tear open the condom's foil. Must seem sordid after years of marriage, like adultery in an unclean motel in broad daylight.

The sorrow of latex, a pitiful fraction of the best feeling in the world. Best one can hope is that she doesn't feel the difference, that she will loosen up as we go, until self-consciousness lifts from us both and we can be happy in our nakedness.

Not yet. Eyes closed, holding onto my back, cooperating instead of enjoying. Move different ways, seek the motion that will touch her.

Have never seen such an absence of response. Unwise, to think I could sweep her troubles away so quickly. Just finish and be done. Move faster, get it over with.

Her mouth opens, a bubble of sound bursts on her lips, "Uhh."

Stop, slow down, prolong!

Too late.

A new experience: regret at the instant of coming. Not even ten seconds of grace.

So, here we are. Pressed together with nothing to say.

"Um—I'd better..."

Side by side on our backs now—just like in movies where the adulterers lie drenched in guilt afterwards. Therefore, change the position. On my side, brush a thigh over hers, back and forth.

"That feels nice," she says, and curls against me, face in my chest, our bent legs interlaced. Holds onto me as I drift further and further away from her, fleeing the scene of the crime.

Thus ends our romance.

She sits up suddenly, hugs her knees. (Could she hear what I was thinking?) Thinner than in August when I saw her in a bathing suit, thin enough to count the ribs. She must regret this even more than I do.

Regret: something we have in common, a path to tenderness. Hand on her back.

"I should go," she says.

"Where to?"

"Brooklyn."

Wonder if she brought the key to their brownstone with just this outcome in mind.

"The wind sounds bad."

She rocks forward and back, just slightly. Not leaving yet, offering me a chance to convince her.

"You could stay here. You should."

Her hand on my thigh. "I feel too awkward," then pushes off, stands up.

A gentleman would say, *You shouldn't feel awkward,* but I don't have it in me.

She picks her panties off the floor, gives them a brisk shake, and sits near my feet to put them on. It's over now. We're getting dressed, putting away the bodies.

At the door, buttoning her coat, "You don't have to come with me, I can hail a cab by myself."

"No, it may take a while because of the storm." Shield her from flying debris: one last service as our weeks of intimacy come to an end.

Down the stairs we go, top of her head below me, scalp visible at her part, that thin hair. Not one glance back at me.

A gust almost blows a seagull into the side of my building. Traffic light over 15th Street swinging and creaking. Here comes her cab, shining yellow, cutting across the avenue to us. Brakes with a squeal.

"Lori—"

Her hand is already on the chrome handle, and I have nothing to say.

"Will you be all right?"

"I'm fine, Burt."

Climbs in without so much as a dry kiss.

Note the driver's name, Mansur Makloufy, in case anything happens to her.

Red tail lights carry her away. Above Gristedes, taped asterisks on many windows. Somewhere, a footnote must explain what happened tonight.

•

White tape on brown skin, oval patch of cotton over Ernie Edwards' injured eye. Smell of liquor and days of accumulated sweat. Ernie in my chair, door closed, Patty shaking his wrist to make him listen, "You had an accident, that's all, it doesn't mean anything more than that." Patty's stern sincerity, trying to get through to him, but his head keeps swaying from side to side. "I'm never gonna read," he says for the tenth time, and I believe he's right, he'll never reach his goal. Just like I'll never have Lori, or any other mate. "I know it feels impossible because it's so far away," Patty says. "But nothing is impossible. You can walk a thousand miles if you keep going one step at a time." If anyone else said that, I'd dismiss it as smiley-face B. S., but with Patty, you have to take it seriously, think about it. Lori: Is it still possible to salvage something? Could be—with struggle—but not if I do a Burt, *commence evasive action,* hide from her and let time bury Tuesday night.

"Look," Patty tells Ernie, "all I'm saying is, don't make your mind up that you're quitting. Give yourself some time off, and then remember that you *have* made progress, and if you're patient, you can go further. Will you promise me?"

His head keeps swaying, he's too far gone to hear, but her words haven't been wasted. This time I won't give up so fast. Tomorrow is Saturday: take the train to Manhasset, surprise Lori. Because even though Ernie has lost his faith, even though I have doubts of my own, I'm willing to gamble that it's possible to grow, to become a bigger person than I've been so far.

•

Rainwater from my soaked sneakers pooling darkly on the concrete porch. Jacket way too thin for the weather, hands wet from doing up the umbrella snap. Lights on in living room, 1001 violins playing "And I Love Her."

Go ahead, despite terror. Ring the bell.

(So suburban. White bird-bath, yellow vinyl siding, different from the garden apartments where I grew up, a higher rung of the middle class.)

Bong bunggggg. *Enter the romantic hero, led in by Mom, soggy sneakers squidging. "Look who's here."*

Gurgle of water from downspout into a puddle in the shrubs. No sounds from inside but the quasi-music. Ring again; again, nothing.

Where would they all go? Annual visit to the cemetery is what comes to mind, though all four of her grandparents are alive.

Take a look around the side. Sheets of rain—umbrella up again—and sloggy grass. Her window would be next to the patio. There: her desk, with paints and brushes. Lights off, no one in, too dark to see what she's working on.

And so ends the story of Burt and Lori.

Back to the station, a mile in wet sneakers. House after house sealed tight against the cold rain, while my umbrella leaks droplets on my head.

Car going the other way stops, backs up. Buick LeSabre, burgundy, Mafia-type car. Keep walking, it probably has nothing to do with me.

"Burt?"

Lori's eyes above the top edge of the back window.

"Hi." Chest thumps, worse than if a thug pointed a gun at me.

"Would you like a ride?"

Climb in, and now I'm dripping on the velour back seat and her flat brown Macy's bag.

"What are you doing here?" she inquires.

Constrained by the listeners in the front seat, "I thought I'd surprise you."

Mrs. F. smiling to herself. *Poor boy has a crush on our Lori.*

Dark wet patch of carpet at my feet. Lori moves the paper bag to her lap, protecting it from my leakage. Her spirit seems intact, in no need of succor from me. Mother chattering, "You must be chilled to the bone, we'll give you some of Ira's old clothes to put on. You should stay for supper, Harold brought home skirt steaks." Lori's hands folded on top of her bag, looking out her window, away from me.

Mistake. Folly. Abort.

Pants, socks and sneakers in the washing machine. Bare feet and too-big jeans. (Her brother must have some rear end.) Leaning back against the closed door while Lori, on the stars-and-snowflakes comforter, snips the plastic filament and price tag from a pair of black leather gloves. "I said I didn't have gloves for the winter, so they rushed me to the store. They think I'll fall apart if they don't attend to my every need."

Through the gauzy curtains, gray light of a rainy afternoon. On the desk, Ned the giraffe stumbling down subway stairs in a derby. Such cheerful whimsy in the midst of turmoil. Such discipline.

Though unwanted, my speech must be made.

"Lori. Do you know why I came out?"

Puts her hands into the black gloves. "To tell me we can still be friends even though we're embarrassed?"

Can't tell if she means she would like that, or I can go to hell with my condescension. Too complicated to guess; just plod onwards.

"Not exactly. I was thinking that we both regretted what happened, but I don't really believe it was a mistake." Slow down, pause for breath. As she stretches her fingers inside the gloves. Is she listening? Just go on. "Of course we're self-conscious, but that doesn't mean we shouldn't try. I still think we could be good together, even if Tuesday night was awkward. We would be crazy to give up so soon. I'm saying that I want to keep seeing you."

Warm and steady Lori gaze again, first in a long time. "Come here." Gloved hand flat on the bed next to her.

Grasp the pants tight at the side, this is no time to have them fall around my knees. Sit in the indicated place, to receive either a kind farewell or *I love you.*

"I thought you just wanted to get rid of me," she says. Giant dark eyes.

"Well, it felt so weird afterwards. But I'm braver now."

"I still don't know if I'm really ready. But I'm willing to try."

Stay cool. Show dignity.

"I think, if we're patient with each other, we can overcome everything."

Smiling to herself, like her mother in the car. Tears in my eyes, because maybe she will love me after all.

"This turned out better than I expected," I say, voice cracking.

Her eyes clear and dry, but affectionate. And then we're lying on the stars and snowflakes, her socks pressed against the tops of my bare feet, warming them. I kiss her, she kisses me: tenderly, eyes open. Seeing how it feels.

(It feels great.)

•

On the wine-red carpet down below, men in dark suits bring plastic champagne glasses to their women. One girl in a backless velvet gown, others calf-length and floral. What I'd like to do is take Lori's small shoulders in my hands and kiss her throat. Don't want to startle her, though.

Her hands on the brass railing. Cover one of hers with one of mine, fingers between fingers.

"Explain something to me. Why do all little girls want to be ballerinas?"

"I didn't. I wanted to be a violinist."

"Ah. Like your father."

Mild smile as she watches a white-haired life-of-the-party reduce his bosomy young companion to giggles.

"So why didn't you pursue it?"

"I'm not sure. I just forgot about it."

A girl as tall as her mother's waist tries a ballet leap, trips on the hem of her dress, tumbles to the carpet and rolls on purpose. Ignored, she runs back and tugs on Mom's sleeve. Imagine she's our daughter. A sweet dream.

But if I want it to come true, I'd better learn how to talk to Lori again. "I get the impression when I watch ballet dancers that their goal is to eliminate human imperfection from their movement."

"Sounds like a fair description."

"No, I mean it's scary. Like they aspire to be machines."

"Does that mean you didn't enjoy the dances?"

Careful here. "I respect the years of work, the discipline that lets them hold a leg out at a right angle—" *But it looks like vain prancing to me.* "I guess as artforms go, I like painting better."

"I didn't love the first piece," she says. "It was just bleak and repetitive. But the second one seemed charming."

And thus she exposes my error: judging from hostile bias instead of evaluating each work on its own merits.

"Did you ever take dance classes? You sound like you must have."

"No, I'm just a fan. But we did take a couple of ballroom dancing lessons once."

We.

A chubby young couple do a few waltz steps below us. In love, at ease.

"Tell me something," I try. "If you could be anything you wanted, what would you be?"

Altered smile, tighter. "Are you interviewing me?"

Twitch of her hand sends mine flying—unnecessarily, she meant nothing by it, her hand's still there. Can't put mine back, though. Not for a while.

The lights should dim any second now, send us back to our seats. A chance to keep quiet, wipe the slate clean. Just pay closer attention to the rest of the dances. Find something intelligent to say.

•

12:03. Faint whistle from her nose, in and out. I can see, in the light from the alley, a crumb at the corner of her mouth. Better leave it, if I don't want to wake her.

Third night together since my soggy visit to Manhasset, and I can't see any progress. Always on our best behavior—even in bed. Sense of unrelenting constraint.

Because, face it, she wasn't ready. Even if she doesn't compare me with Alan every minute, which she must, there's no way she could transfer her love so swiftly. Just as Patty predicted.

A stirring at my side. Feels me awake, sidles closer, presses her behind against my hip. Affection, more precious than gold.

Kiss her shoulder, as I've wanted to so many times but couldn't.

Her eyes open, seeing me. Compressed smile: her daytime face. "Can't sleep?"

"Mm."

Hold her, my front against her back. Smell her hair. (While I still can.)

•

Dinner table + bridge table + white paper tablecloth = Thanksgiving. Two parents, two brothers, two sisters-in-law, two plump nieces in green kilts; and Lori, and me, the supposedly platonic friend.

From carving of turkey to painful bloating in just 25 minutes. Mostly-empty serving dishes of wrinkly baked potatoes, julienne string beans with sliced almonds, noodle kugel, cranberry-sauce slices, and sweet potato mush topped with browned mini-marshmallows. Brothers comparing notes on their new cars, Mercury Sable versus Saturn. Lori's father slouching and ashen, possibly brooding over his lost son-in-law, or else fighting off a heart attack from overeating. The sisters-in-law rave about a new musical Lori *must* see, "It's so exhilarating!" (Only a few years older than us, but they talk like my mother.) Everyone has taken a turn distracting Lori on this first holiday without a husband, and she has shown heroic interest in each piece of chatter they've aimed at her.

Nothing left for me to do but sulk. Not that I want to announce our tenuous connection and face their disapproval over the sweet potatoes, but I can't seem to find anything, uh, exhilarating in her keeping us a secret.

Morty, the younger brother, asks if I have a car and I

answer, "No, I live in Manhattan." Not intended as a witticism, but he takes it that way, laughing hospitably, which only makes me tired.

Ira and Morty hoist themselves out of their chairs to watch the football game. "Come on, Dad, if Miami wins, the Giants are in first place."

"I hate those Cowboys," but he rises anyway, speed of a glacier.

"You a Giants fan, Burt?" asks Ira, the humorless but prosperous pet shop owner.

Use tact, just in case I have a future here. "Yeah, but I'm too stuffed to move. I'll come in a few minutes."

With the three Mr. Feigs gone, Lori's mother sighs, signal for the women to clean up. (What has changed here since 1965? Not much.) I collect as many used paper napkins as I can without leaving my seat; I'm in no mood to have Lori's mother scold me for helping.

"Why are you putting all the napkins on your plate?" asks the taller of the two nieces.

"I have a collection at home."

"Whaaaa?"

Unloving in my gloom, I have no interest in these kids. Ignore them.

Stamped into the paper tablecloth are countless ridges, like long-grain rice. They could be fallen soldiers covered with snow, viewed from 1,000 feet up.

Here's Lori again, excused. "Want to go to my room?"

"Could we come too?" asks the big niece.

"No, I want to talk to Burt. I'll play with you later."

Puts her little chin in her palms dramatically to show disappointment, but doesn't argue.

Past the wall of 8x10s, Lori and Ira and Morty through the years, with braces, accordions, a schnauzer. Between the two brothers' wedding pictures, one of Lori, younger, alone. Impossible to imagine a picture of Lori and me there.

Just inside her doorway, out of everyone's sight, Lori hugs me. Soak in the warmth of her body, and conceal the surprise.

"How are you doing?" I ask.

"I'll survive. What about you?"

Shrug.

"Can I cheer you up?" she says, glint in her eye, wiggle of her behind. A Lori I barely recognize.

And so we kiss standing up, door left open recklessly, a wild pair. Bring her snugly against me, by her small but adorable behind.

Stampede of quick little feet on carpet. Flash of a white anklet, and five-inch shoe of black patent leather.

Still linked, we stare where the feet were a moment ago. Listen for tattletale whispers, but hear none. The Cowboys score, the Feig men curse.

Closing her door, Lori says, "It's all right if they tell, as long as you're not planning to break up with me right away. That would be too humiliating."

"I promise not to break up with you before you break up with me."

She leads me by the hand behind the open closet door, hiding place from sudden intruders. "Now where were we?"

Squeeze her, to make sure she's real.

Half-time is dessert time. Back to the table, new paper tablecloth. "Miami's lost without Marino," mutters Ira as he plops down into the chair. "You have to give the Cowboys credit," Morty counters, "What an offense."

Mr. Feig staring hard at his cake plate, either because he knows and can't bear to look at Lori and me, or because of an unrelated preoccupation. His wife slicing the pumpkin pie with angry eyes, the sisters-in-law hiding in their china cups of decaf. Uh-oh. As my father never told me but should have, Hold your head up, son. Whatever happens, do not cringe.

Mrs. Feig's knife scrapes against the pie tin. Acid glance at Lori, who deflects it with a non-responsive smile.

"Mom, did you make this pie or did you buy it?" asks Morty's wife.

"Buy it, are you kidding?" Morty says. "This is her world-famous recipe, she won a prize at temple."

"Yeah yeah yeah," Mrs. Feig mutters.

Ira to everyone, "Did you see on the news about that lunatic who shot three drivers—"

"*Ira*," his wife whines.

"What?"

Nods at the girls, who are too young to hear such things. "The guy on the Expressway overpass," he continues. "It happened three blocks from the store. We heard the shots, I thought somebody was setting off cherry bombs."

"There were shots outside my office building last year," says Morty. "I never heard gunshots before, but I instantly knew what they were."

Ira, "What a genius."

Morty on the defensive, "No, I mean you'd think my first thought would be, *fireworks*, but it's interesting that it wasn't."

Ira rolls his eyes, and now the brothers are too annoyed to talk to each other. (That's what Thanksgiving is for, the reawakening of ancient enmities.) All we have for distraction is the Ford commercial on the TV they left on. Mrs. Feig giving me the evil eye, as if Lori's problems were all my fault.

"Burt, would you pass me that sugar?" says Morty, the innocent.

"Here you go."

Lori seeks my hand under the table, hidden by the paper cloth, and squeezes it. She whispers, "I think I'd like to stay with you in the city tonight."

Nod. Rub her pinky with my thumb. My Lori.

While tears gather at her father's red eyelids.

Goodbye to Alan after all.

9.

AFTER-WORK CHRISTMAS shoppers blocking my way, trudging along this narrow trench between ankle-high banks of melting ice. Alan in trouble—his secretary's panicked murmur over the phone, "He's *crying* in there!" Either Suzanne broke her vow and deserted him, or he's going to prison. Not sure which is worse.

His building: dismal lobby, dingy brown marble, overpowering smell of printer's ink. Inviting as a morgue.

Peg—23, Irish from Queens, flat and wide like a kite, we used to joke and flirt on the phone until we met and disappointed each other—jumps out from behind her desk to whisper, "He said through the door that I could go home, but I couldn't. I never heard him like this. He's losing it."

Smudged mascara, crying because he's crying. Devoted to him: she brings him homemade brownies. A reminder that he's a good guy more often than not, that I've looked up to him more than I've resented him.

From behind his door, a cough. She flinches, and her giant engagement ring flashes. "He keeps breaking down in tears. I was afraid to leave him alone."

"I'll stay with him. Thanks for calling me."

She takes her coat (tan and white fur) from the simple black rack. Confidentially, "I just hope he goes back to his wife. She's the one he belongs with."

"Mm."

The door closes harder than she probably meant it to. Extremely quiet all of a sudden. He must be listening from inside to see if she's gone.

I should move around, make noise, let him know I'm here. Not ready to face him, though.

On the wall, a magnetic chart headed *December Rent*, the *December* floating on a blue cloud of erased months. A row for each of his rental units, and a round red magnet moved to the PAID column on all but six rows. Desk cluttered with pink post-it notes (*Ft. Greene #31 moving 2/1*) and small manila coin envelopes bulging with keys. His business is as straightforward as a hot-dog stand. So remote from intellect—so different from any ambition of mine.

Beyond the door, his leather couch crunches, a sitting-down sound. Then something else, like a wooden house creaking—no, it's him, a crushed moan that keeps going, going, until it crumbles into crying like a child's.

At last, relief, the crying subsides into wet sniffling. But not for long. Loud heaving grunts, guts pouring out.

Stop him. Knock.

When he finally hears me knocking, the noise shuts off instantly. "It's Burt. Can I come in?"

Couch sound again, standing up, but no footsteps. Composing himself in the mirror?

Door opens on red eyes and wrinkled white shirt. Needs a shave, and smells like chicken soup. Suitcase of clothes open on the black leather couch: contrast of antiseptic furniture and disorderly socks. Garment bag hanging on the door; chaotic files littering the black marble desktop.

He gambled everything he had, and lost.

Wipes the remaining tears from his eyes fast. Puts hands in pants pockets, impersonating a casual host. "What's going on?" he asks.

"Peg called me. She was worried about you."

Annoyed frown. He'd prefer me not to refer to his condition, I'm ruining the pretense of normalcy. Invites me to take off my down jacket and knapsack. "Have a seat," indicating the couch, but first he must close the suitcase to make room. Goes behind the desk, sits in the oxblood leather chair—Wall Street/Gatsby style that doesn't go with the rest of the room.

He hunches forward with chin hidden behind meshed fingers, too tired to sit up straight. Between my calves, my knapsack slumps over as if losing heart. Since I have no counseling skills, bluntness will have to do. "What happened?"

"We had a talk. I decided to move out."

I'm skeptical that it was his decision, but suspend judgment. "When was this?"

Counts backwards in his mind. "The night before last."

"And you've been sleeping here, on the couch?"

Nods soberly, protecting his dignity.

"What did she say? Unless you don't want to talk about it."

Leans back and sinks down into the chair, a foot of leather backrest above his head. "We had problems. She would go a whole night without saying a word to me. I finally asked her if there was anything I could do to make it work." The memory makes him smile—the screaming smile of one whose hand has just been sliced off.

"She said No?"

Takes him a few moments to get control of his voice again. "She never said she wanted to break up. She even said she would go ahead with the wedding if I wanted to. Sick, right?"

Don't answer.

"Know what's funny? While we were talking, I could handle everything very rationally. It was a relief to get it out in the open. We even agreed about how close we felt to each other—I don't think we ever talked that honestly before. But once I had all my things in the car..."

I can just see him: stumbling down the front steps with suitcase and garment bag, throwing up between his car and the curb.

He notices how low he has sunk in the chair, and straightens up. Looking at the palm of his hand, like Mom did at Dad's funeral.

"So, you don't have any place to shower?"

"I'll probably move into one of my vacant apartments."

Despite the *Lori Lori Lori* pounding in my head, "Why don't you come stay with me?"

"That's all right, I just need to buy a bed and some things, then I'll be set."

"You can do that over the weekend. Make it easy on

yourself, just for a few nights. My apartment is only a few blocks away."

Nudges the edge of a file folder parallel with the edge of the desk. "It might not be a bad idea. I have a meeting with my lawyer in the morning."

"What about?"

"It's complicated. The government is subpoenaing some information about a loan application. The lawyer wants to see everything in my files."

All this and prison too. "Come on, you'll feel better when you take a shower and eat something."

He's wandering back into himself, though. Neck sinking down into his shoulders.

"What are you thinking?"

"It's all because I hurt Lori."

Impatiently (and maybe that's good, a bracing slap), "It's not punishment, don't go flaky. You did a brave thing, you reached for what you always wanted. You didn't do it to be selfish, or to hurt her—you thought you belonged with Suzanne."

All of which I sort of believe, though for the last ten minutes I've been judging him a fool for making the same mistake twice.

He's less convinced than I am, however. Opens the bottom drawer of his desk, takes out a framed 5x7, sets it on the blotter and stares into it. Lori, no doubt.

"Let's go outside, Alan. You need fresh air."

"I'm wiped. Give me a minute to stretch out on the couch."

Trade places. (Not Lori on his desk, but their wedding picture.) He moves the suitcase to the floor and lies on the sofa. In less than a minute he's snoring, the same slobbery noise that used to keep me awake when we shared a room.

Files open in front of me. RPIE form, NYC Department of Finance, might shed light on his problems if I could decode it. At one corner of the desk, a tall silver pyramid, his idea of a mogul's knickknack. Such grand ambitions—and so crass.

His hand drops to the carpet and lies there. Slain.

Last time, when he found her note ("She's going to Russia," he told me, immobilized in the kitchen with an apple in his other hand) he didn't cry right away. Then I followed a banging sound into his bedroom, where he was sitting on the floor, hitting his head sideways against the wall. He wasn't hitting the wall hard enough to hurt himself, just beating time, applying counterpressure to the pain; but he didn't stop or slow down, not even when he saw me in the doorway. I said, "Don't do that," which had no effect. In the end I had to pull him away from the wall, taking the risk that he would lash out at me. Instead he went passive, let me help him up and lead him away. Seemed to want me to *keep* leading him, out of his room and out of his suffering—which was so far beyond my ability that I abdicated, led him no further than his bed, told him, "You should rest." He obeyed, curled up on his side as Lori did the night of the hurricane, and covered his head with a pillow. Taking the kitchen phone out the back door, I called our school's suicide hotline, just in case. The girl on the other end sounded younger than me, but pompous, which reassured me, let me believe she knew more than I did. She said not to leave him alone, and to encourage him to talk about his feelings. I went back to his room and sat at the foot of the bed, hi-liting a book about Australian aborigines for an anthro midterm. When he woke up, thrashing, I asked how he was doing and he said he wanted to get drunk. So, despite my misgivings, we poured the last three inches from a vodka bottle into a half-full quart of orange juice; in twenty minutes, he drank all but one glass of it, while I groped for reassuring words. "Better now than after you got married," I said, and although it was true, the lameness of it made me wince. (At least I did better than Ugly, who advised Alan, "Women are like buses, there'll be another one along any minute.") Next he was staggering out of the house, swaying down the street toward the campus in his white socks, even though there were still patches of snow on the ground. I followed with his shoes, letting him stay a few yards ahead, since he seemed to want to be by himself. He ducked into a grove of trees in the town park—trying to lose me, I thought, but then a car turning a corner lit him up, on one knee, arm around a tree trunk. When the light was gone, I found him by the sound of his retching. I slept in my sleeping bag on his bedroom floor that night, without asking permission or explaining myself; he was too out of it to argue. In the morning he seemed calmer, though bleary-eyed. He insisted I didn't have to worry about him, he just wanted to go back to sleep. I considered skipping my midterm to stay with him, but he convinced me there was no need, so I went to school, and when I came home that afternoon I found blood on the kitchen table and floor, and the window jagged. I thought he was dead, and had already dialed 911 when our gregarious neighbor stopped by to tell me how he had seen Alan's arm hanging through the window, etc., etc.

My fault, for leaving him alone. But I'll do better this time. This time he won't get out of my sight.

8:30, starving. Only thirteen blocks from home, and trapped without food.

Solution: Charlie Mom delivers.

Out to Peg's desk to call in the order without waking him. Foot-tall Christmas tree with miniature presents underneath, brass clothespin for messages, *Mrs. Waites, DeKalb #5, son in hospital, will pay next week. Nice lady, I told her okay. Okay?*

When I return, he asks blankly, "What?"

Eyes closed, possibly dreaming.

"Who were you talking to?" he asks, blinking.

"I ordered Chinese food. You want to share it?"

"I'm not hungry. Let me sleep some more."

And so he does, on his side now, nose against the black leather of the back cushion, a way to see nothing even if his eyes happen to open.

Back to my anatomy and physiology book. (But

Lori—our nightly call, if he's with me I won't be able to speak, and how will I explain that, to her and to him, and what if she calls when I'm in the bathroom and he picks up the phone, or worse, *doesn't* pick up and hears her leave a message? If I could just get out of earshot for two minutes, I could call her and lie that I have to go out of town, my mother's sick in L.A. Deceit, that's what's needed.)

Not easy to concentrate on the workings of the pancreas.

The bell, an old nagging buzzer. Chinese guy in a yellow rainsuit, snowdrops on his glasses. Alan on his feet again, sets me up at Peg's desk with a red plastic plate and heavy flatware, better than I use at home.

Uncomfortable eating in the company of someone who's not, especially when he's rubbing his forehead, massaging away a headache and shaming me for having an appetite at all. Finish fast; slurp up that watercress.

Alan insists on carrying the suitcase and garment bag, leaving me nothing to hold but his shopping bag of toiletries. In the elevator, he slumps against the side wall, something I've never seen him do before.

Out the lobby door into the cold. Snowflakes in our faces, reminder of long ago, a forgotten pleasure. Pair of beautiful Korean children bundled up in bright snowsuits, Mom shepherding them from behind with harsh words. Alan oblivious, watching the slush climb the sides of his new shoes.

Christmas trees for sale, incongruous scent of pine needles. Gray-haired young woman in lumberjack plaid and a Santa hat, a hardy sort, blowing into her hands, and here comes her husband, less good-natured, maybe because no one's buying. Hands her a paper cup of coffee, she takes the lid off, steam rises.

Alan sets down suitcase and garment bag in the slush, goes to the window of a closed drugstore, leans forehead and hands against the glass. Get him away from there before he puts a hand through.

But first bring his bags over, don't let a thief walk away with them. "Alan? It's going to be all right."

Panting, with tears or mucus hanging from his nose. A croak, "I hurt Lori so bad."
Hand on his back. He turns, throws his arms around me. Rub his back, "It's okay." Throbbing chest, a feeling like love.
"I appreciate her so much now."
The lumberjack husband watching us. Probably thinking, *Faggots.*
"There's a bar across the street, let's stop there for a minute. I'll buy you a drink."
Doesn't want to let go. "I can never make it up to her. We just don't belong together."
I'll rejoice later. "Come on, you should sit down."
Ease myself out of his embrace, and take all three of his bags. He follows me tamely across Seventh Avenue. Hurry—light just changed, here come the cabs, charging like bulls.
Into the dark and smoke. Skinny bartender holding a tap as beer fills a mug. Empty except for a crowd of young sales rep types, trenchcoats folded on barstools, ties loosened, Monday Night Football on the TV—Cowboys versus a helmet I don't recognize. "Lame Jerk!" someone barks, and another one says, "There's his friend, Blow Job." On the screen, a ref with the letters *BJ* on the back of his striped shirt. Okay, I get it, nothing to do with us.
Give Alan the side of the booth facing the TV, reverse view in the wall-mirror for me. Keeps his wet coat on, somberly watches a replay of Leon Lett's bouncing belly.
Tall old waiter in white shirt and string tie clomps over to us, ash-gray face, impatient. Scotch on the rocks for me, but Alan has a hard time deciding. Finally asks for a margarita. Waiter sneers, barely perceptibly.
"Somehow that isn't what I expected you to order."
Twitch of a shrug, and now I remember: margaritas are what Lori always orders in a bar.
He's barely breathing. Startle him awake.
"I can't tell if you're depressed about Suzanne or about Lori."

Ignores the question and glances up at the screen as a punted ball spins end over end, falling from the sky into the hands of a small player in yellow, who darts between defenders like a minnow. Someone's got his ankle but he wriggles free, outmaneuvering them for forty yards. Distant memory: this is what I once dreamed of becoming, the nimble punt returner who slips between the giants, evades their meaty hands, zigs and zags and never lets them catch him. (Though now he's down—and before he can stand, a Cowboy gives him a quick kick in the face-mask, unseen by the refs.) On the replay one of the after-work guys says, "Looks like Danz running to the john after his morning muffin." Danz replies, "If I wanted abuse, I could stay home with my wife."

Here come the drinks, short glass of mostly ice cubes for me, big festive goblet for Alan. "I've got it," say I, reaching into my pocket. He doesn't protest. Sunk low in the wooden booth seat, he acknowledges neither the waiter nor me.

Condensation on the round bowl of his glass trickles slowly down to the stem.

"Alan, talk to me. What are you thinking about?"

His lips part, but only a bubble comes out. Pop.

"When was the last time you ate? I know you're not hungry, but you'll collapse if you don't eat. Let's get you a burger."

He looks up at the game. Slow-motion running back uses an old-fashioned stiff-arm on a linebacker's helmet, looks like the linebacker's neck has snapped. "Boingggggg," says one of the trenchcoat guys.

Alan gets up, walks away from the booth.

"Where are you going?"

"Men's room."

Can't follow him, probably one of those one-bowl broom closets. Just keep track of the time, 9:22. If he hasn't come back by 9:27, go after him.

Raise a hand for the waiter, to ask if they make burgers here, but he's leaning on the bar and watching the game, either doesn't see or doesn't want to be bothered. "Christ," one of the salesmen mumbles, because there's a player writhing on his back, one leg bent—uh-oh, the leg is bent the wrong way, sideways. Look away, down into my scotch, get that picture out of my mind. Frank Gifford narrates the replay, "There's Washington coming in from the left, and watch Everett come in the other way. Oh boy. This is not pretty."

"Kiss that sucker's career goodbye."

Honking outside, damn cabbies. What's going on? Ah, some drunk's crossing Seventh Avenue against the light—no, not a drunk, *Alan,* sleepwalking among the yellow cars.

Out into the falling snow—blaring horns, cabs veering around him, and he's floating, head tipped back, not even noticing them—no opening for me in the rush of cars—now? no—*now,* behind the white van, fast, get to him—grab his arm, slipping on slush, no traction—snow wet on his dark hair, eyes squinted shut—slow-moving, not refusing to go, just dragging as if we were under water. "Come on, Alan, hurry"—angry horns, and one cab coming at us, swerving in a skid—shove him between the parked cars, and he stumbles into the fender—the cab coming at me passenger side first, can't get my footing, if the bad knee gets hit I doubt they'll be able to repair it again—but that couldn't happen—

Yow—ankle-bone struck by lightning.

Falling, powerless to stop it, not as nimble and invulnerable as I thought.

Did I black out? Don't think so. Strangely, the pain is gone. Oily ice shines darkly under a streetlight, dirty rivulet flows into a curbside stream, which I'm lying across.

"Burt?"

On his knees, cold hand on my forehead, but in his eyes, nothing. No remorse, no care.

Someone else next to him. "I hardly touched him. This is unfuckingbelievable."

The cabbie: our age and size, but the similarity ends

there. Long-johns shirt, sleeves pushed up, Marine Corps insignia tattooed on forearm.

"What were you doing out there? What are you, stoned?"

My pants are wet, my palms are scraped. Rotate the throbbing foot, see if it moves. Yes, and still pointing the right way.

We're by the Christmas trees again. Dusted with snow, could be in the woods, in Canada. That scent, so beautiful.

"Ask him if he's hurt. Are you hurt?"

"I'm okay."

Then prove it, stand up. Cabbie seizes my arm roughly, Alan takes the other one. Cold water dripping down the inside of my pants.

Test the foot. Take a step. More lightning, but tolerable. "I'll be fine. Let's just get to my apartment."

Alan, "You should have an X-ray."

"I can walk, I don't need an X-ray."

As if his soul had already left him, Alan gives in without argument. Cabbie asks where I live, then offers us a ride, building goodwill to fend off a personal injury suit. So now we're in Lawrence Bartnick's cab, silent threesome. Can't say I resent Alan's unconcern for me—he thought he was going to die, after all—but his selfish passion is a different matter. Repulsive: endangering other people because he can't rein in his colossal feelings. Everyone else holds something back, protects at least the inner core of the heart from breaking, but not him. And not just now; always.

Hands limp in his lap, without even the strength to knit his fingers. Nullifying my complaint.

Bartnick carries the luggage as far as the doorstep. "You take care of yourself," and then he's gone, fled.

Take the narrow steps one at a time, Alan behind me. Exaggerate the pained limp, feign helplessness, because he won't try it again as long as I need him. (I think.)

"Ow, shit. Could I lean on you?"

Mute as a laboring ox, he allows it.

Light on, quick scan for signs of Lori—photos, earrings,

giraffe-doodles?—but there are none, except the blinking indicator on the answering machine. While he, stuck three feet from the door, bags still in his hands, waits for me to tell him what to do. Doesn't even look like himself. It's like someone drove a spike through the personality center of his brain.

"Could you spread a towel over that chair for me? I don't want to get it filthier than it already is."

Nods, fetches from bathroom—quick, pull the plug on the answering machine, before he says, *You have a message*—and lays the blue towel over the armchair. Now I can hang up my jacket and collapse. Rub the ankle cautiously through the pantsleg. Feels hot. Alan next to the dinner table, swaying. "Why don't you hang up your garment bag? I'll clear some space in the closet for you."

"You don't have to."

"I realize there's no legal obligation, but."

No smile. Zombies don't banter.

"At least take off your coat."

He obeys, hangs it next to my jacket, sleeve against oil-smeared sleeve, and stops to look at my parents kissing. Same photo Lori examined, hurricane night.

"Yes?"

"I didn't say anything."

"I mean, what are you thinking about the picture?"

Focuses more intently. Then shrugs.

I need to pee, but fear to leave him alone and idle. "There's a foam mattress in the closet, up on the shelf. Maybe you can get it down and set it up on the floor."

Go fast, while he complies.

Quick check of the medicine chest: no razor blades, no prescription drugs, good. He'd have to hang himself from the shower rod with dental floss. Anyway, not likely that he'd kill himself in my home, not after messing me up this much.

He's on hands and knees, unrolling the yellowed foam between bed and bookcase, only place it fits. Kneeling on the curling end to keep it flat. Catatonic, but at least he's alive.

Hand him a sheet from the closet, and sleeping bag to use as blanket. Gray face as he unfolds the sheet, which worries me. Unless I get through to him, he may leave while I'm asleep and try it again.

"Do you want to talk about Suzanne?"

"No. Thanks."

Goes on making his bed, tucking each side under the foam. Finished, he sits on it, facing the bookcase, not me. "I wasn't in love with her this time," he says. "She was different than I remembered. A lot harder. I thought she would change if I stayed with her—but she didn't."

Keep him talking. "You looked pretty involved."

"I kept believing we had a future. But she has such a merciless way of looking at people. She sees every fault."

Makes me wince to imagine the things she told him about himself. About me.

"I feel bad for her," he says. "I think she's going to end up alone."

"It's good that you can see all this. I didn't think you did."

Contemplative silence, head bowed. Opportunity for me to sit down, give the foot a rest. Behind my desk—not too close, give him room.

"How are you doing?" I ask.

"Mm."

"You sound a little better. At least you're talking."

No answer. Humming sound, what is it? My clock.

"Would you mind if I just went to sleep?" he says.

Should keep him talking, but how, how, how? "Whatever you want."

In all these years, I've never seen him naked and he hasn't seen me. Nor will it happen tonight: I hobble into the bathroom to change from dirty damp clothes to gym shorts, and when I come out, he's climbing into the sleeping bag in his white briefs.

I guess it's all right, on a night when he tried to kill himself and I got hit by a car, to skip brushing our teeth.

"Are you still going to go to your meeting in the morning? With the lawyer?"

"I don't know." Takes the pillow I hand him. "I'd probably better."

Which means I should go with him, if this is to be different from last time. Just need to figure out something to say that will justify my sticking to him like a Secret Service agent.

"What time do you want to get up?"

"Eight o'clock."

Set the alarm. Into the kitchen to pick up two empty Pepsi cans, then shut the overhead light and silently stack the cans against the door, to hear if he tries to sneak out. (If he asks why in the morning: *To remind me to take them back for the deposit.*)

Careful on the way back, don't step on his face.

Lying in the dark, separate. I must say something, because as of now, he may still dive in front of a subway train tomorrow.

"Alan?"

"Huh?"

"There are a lot of people who care about you." Sudden constriction in my throat, and also no idea what more to say. "What you're going through, it'll get better with time. You won't always feel this bad."

"I know."

(Meaning, possibly, *The pain will all be gone tomorrow.*)

"Do you think . . . I don't want to offend you, but do you think you're past the point where you'd try anything like that again?"

"Yes. Let's just go to sleep, all right?"

"Okay."

On our backs, parallel and still, the edge of the bed screening him from my sight. Snuffling through his nose, congested from earlier crying. We've done this before:

lying awake in the dark, close but separate, swimming in emotion.

When? In our dorm room?

No. The end of our Southern trip, after graduation. When we lay next to each other on a mothball-smelling motel bed in Virginia, me in my sleeping bag. The night before we were to drive home to our post-collegiate lives. Him depressed about the job he was about to start, me grieving because we'd just spent ten days together and I didn't want to lose his company. A unique trip for us—after Suzanne, before Lori, the one time when neither of us had a girlfriend. Enclosed in his dented, 150,000-mile car, which miraculously made it over the Smoky Mountains, through Atlanta and New Orleans, across Alabama and back through Virginia. That night when I drove and he slept, and the sun came up over the bald brown Tennessee hills, unlike any place I'd ever seen, and I tapped his knee with one fingertip to wake him, so he could see too.

"Hey," I murmur, back in the present. "You awake?"

"Yes."

Deep, quiet voice, as if summoned from the bottom of the sea.

"I was thinking about our trip down south. Remember when we changed the tire in that Winn-Dixie parking lot?"

"Mm."

Black kids sitting on a cinder-block wall, cackling at us for not knowing how, because we jacked up the car before loosening the nuts, and so the wheel kept turning away from the tire iron, until a woman in a pickup called out to us, explaining our mistake.

"Do you remember what the kids yelled?"

"No."

"'Dumb crackers.'"

No reply.

"And what did you yell back?"

He's not cooperating. Not even a *What?*

"You said, 'We're not crackers, we're Heebs.'"

Still no response, but keep trying. What else?

The causeway, somewhere in Louisiana, two narrow lanes straight as a pipe for over two miles in the pouring rain. Alan driving in Zen concentration, never veering from the double yellow line, even when eighteen-wheelers roared by the other way. My awe at his ability to drive so fearlessly straight with so little distance between us and a head-on collision.

No, what we need is something funny. "What about Williamsburg?" I say.

"The Boy Scouts?"

Yes, good, he remembers. A thousand khaki uniforms mobbing the blacksmith's, the candle-dipping shop, the toilets. Pimples everywhere, and uniformed scoutmasters too, with pale hairy knees. Alan and me unshaven, in wrinkled T-shirts, camping dirt in our hair. The boys kept peeking at us—no way to tell whether they envied our freedom or prayed they wouldn't look like us when they grew up.

"Did you actually say to them, 'Hey, want to buy some drugs?' Or was that an aside to me?"

"I don't remember that at all."

Wish I could detect a grain of pleasure, but can't. "What about the Shoney's in Nashville, the waitress with yellow hair a foot tall?"

"The only thing I remember is the Baltimore jail."

Which makes complete sense. Me driving, him with most of a sixpack in him, tossing firecrackers out the window in the bright afternoon, even after I asked him to stop. Drinking because we would be back home in a few hours, and on Monday he would start a dull job with a tax firm in Queens, commuting from his parents' house in Elmont. No more Suzanne, nothing to look forward to for the rest of his life.

"I said something that pissed the cops off."

"They wanted to let us go, but you said, 'That tin badge don't make you a man.' "

"I was a stupid prick," he mutters.

He may be right—though I've always told it as the funniest story I know. (They handcuffed him, had no interest in me, but I said I'd better come along. "Whatever you want," the cop said, and pulled my plastic handcuffs sadistically tight.)

"Why did I wake up the next morning with eggs all over the floor?" he asks.

"Because they handed us styrofoam plates at five a.m. and you fell back to sleep with yours in your hand."

Facing each other all night in one-man cells, hole in a bench for a toilet. Black guy in the cell next to him, I asked what he did and he mumbled, "Nothing," which made me think *murder*.

The biggest experience of my life: Alan and Burt, ten days out of college, go directly to jail. The charge: Pyrotechnics 3.

"I never apologized for dragging you into trouble," he says.

"Yes you did, but you didn't have to." Keep going, don't chicken out. "What about the night before that, the motel in Virginia?"

"What about it?"

"Did it seem weird to you, that I moved my sleeping bag onto your bed?"

"Maybe, a little. It's hard to remember."

"I did it because I missed you already." And needed to stay close, even if it made him wonder about me.

Clock humming on the desk by my head. No comment from Alan, until: "That was a good trip."

"The best in my life."

Swelling in the chest. If only we could prolong this, preserve it.

"I'm sorry about your foot," he says. "I didn't expect you to come after me."

Swivel the ankle. Stiffening, should probably put ice on it. "I'll be fine."

"You've been a better friend to me than I've been to you."

At last, at long last. My reward.

"We have different talents." Or no, don't leave it at that. "You've given me more happy times than I can count."
Your turn, Alan. Say something else. Keep it going.
"Good night," he says.
Floorboards creak beneath him as he turns over.
"Good night."
I roll onto my side and wait for sleep, wide-eyed.

10.

BITTER COLD OUTSIDE, but warm and haven-like in here, in our comfortable sweatshirts and jeans, Lori with white turtleneck beneath, an appealing collegiate look. Slices of lemon left in the pan, yellow wheels with spokes, flecked with basil and oregano. For such a thin chef, she makes such rich meals. Push the chicken bones from plate into garbage, "I didn't leave you any leftovers."
"You glutton." Rinsing off her plate, grains of brown rice swirling down the drain. And there I am, reflected in the granite countertop, pleasantly swaying from two glasses of wine. Sense that we've made it over the hump, despite her parents' discouraging remarks after Thanksgiving, despite the awkward night when I told her about Alan and Suzanne's breakup and she pretended it didn't matter but then I found her downstairs at three a.m. drinking sherry in the dark. We both seem to want the same thing, to be good to each other, to protect each other from hurt and loneliness. Tonight I'll take the next step, no more waiting: before we go to bed, I will bring up the subject of my moving in. Here comes the future, better than expected.
"What should we do first?" she asks, drying her hands.
"The fire, so we'll have it while we hang the paintings."
"All right, and save the guitar for last. My reward."
Forgot, I agreed to give her an acoustic serenade, a first in my history, because if she can finally hang her paintings, then I can get over my self-consciousness. Still, a touch of dread.
Salad dressing goes back into the door of the gigantic refrigerator ("It's bigger than both of us," I said earlier, earning a smirk of a laugh) and now into the living room we go. A silver pyramid like the one in Alan's office stands on the mantelpiece, but I've learned to ignore these emblems of him. Yes, this was his home, but I'm here now.
Lori kneels on the hearth-bricks, crumples a few sheets

of newspaper, stuffs them under the black grate. Not much for me to do, having no knowledge of fires, just stand to the side and admire her ability. Long matches, crackle of burning paper. "To Build a Fire," that story where the guy freezes to death in the Yukon. My amazement in seventh grade that someone could describe what it felt like to die. What was it like? Not so bad. Like falling asleep.

Lori poking the logs, rearranging them. Framed posters on the floor on either side of her, leaning against the wall under their own paint-shadows. On the mantelpiece with the pyramid are the dried flowers I brought last week; gone are *The Iliad* and *The Odyssey*, tooled leather ugliness, decoration, not literature.

Lori sits on the heels of her moccasins, poker across her thighs, placidly smiling at the new fire. But the crooked end of the smile tips me off that this is a bittersweet reverie. No use asking what she's thinking, she never tells.

"Lori?"

"Hm?"

"I'll bring the paintings up from the basement."

"Thanks."

Down into the chill. Careful, steep steps. First time down here since the night we moved the refrigerator. And there's the pool table, just like in the Feig basement. Lori's father loved Alan, has no fondness for me. I'll just have to live with that—like the furnishings.

Her paintings. Quick survey in the light of one bare bulb: suburban house in snow with zebra peeking in, my favorite; abandoned game of solitaire on dew-damp lawn; lemon, old woman, clock. Nailheads tacking canvas to stretcher, unevenly spaced, she must have stretched them herself. Another skill to admire.

And what do I bring to this match? Only my care for her, which I will prove by protecting these paintings from all things jagged and sharp as I carry them up the steps, two canvases at a time. A test: I must not mar a single painting, not in the slightest, or she will not be mine.

No hands to hold the rail, and the steps seem steeper

going up. Wine-stumble, *careful.* Can still smell the paint—watch out, don't smear it on my pants.

Success. The first two, anyway. Hold up the little zebra painting where I've wanted to hang it, over the round kitchen table. Good, beautiful.

Actually, I'd better wait before bringing the others up, let the alcohol wear off. Discretion, the better part of valor.

Her thin back, and the smell of burning wood. Delicateness of her shoulders, fragility. Want to touch her, but even now, she's beyond my reach.

Kiss the back of her neck. She shivers.

Kneel on the oval rug next to her, shape hands around the fire's warmth. Hard floor even through the rug, but otherwise cozy to the point of luxury. "Is this room available for subletting?"

"Be my guest."

Mistake. Do not jest about what's serious.

"What if we forgot about the paintings," she says, "and made passionate love by the fire?"

The problem is the irony in that word *passionate.* She knows that's not how it would be. Not between us.

"Floor's a mite cold, don't you think?"

"We could put a blanket down."

Bravely looking me in the face. She's trying to overcome our unacknowledged problem, bless her. Even if I don't believe this is the way, I would be a cad not to cooperate. "All right. As long as it's not an itchy blanket."

Hollow metal bang out front, sounds like the gate blown against the old battered trash can. Deserted winter street, forlorn as a prairie train whistle, delivering melancholy into our sanctuary.

And then, the doorbell.

She goes to the end of the couch, leans over, and twists the wand to open the blinds. Outside, under the caged yellow bulb, Alan huddles in his dark coat, steam coming from his nose. Sees her, sees the fire and me. Sunken eyes, just-cut hair exposing red ears. Three weeks since he left my apartment and he looks ten pounds underweight.

He still doesn't know about Lori and me.

She goes around to the entrance hall without comment. Calm and resigned, as if she'd been expecting this.

(Colossal relief that we weren't tangled naked on the floor. Although if we were, she wouldn't have answered the door and he would have gone away unseen. A lesson to me.)

Stand—grip chair for balance—and go to the hallway. Back her up, despite fear.

"I was showing an apartment nearby," he says, out of sight outside the door. "I thought you were staying at your parents'."

He was showing an apartment—even though his closest building is a mile away, with a drug zone in between.

"I moved back a few weeks ago," she explains, neither hostile nor friendly but holding him completely out. A mighty fortress is our Lori.

The cold air from outside makes me shiver.

"Could I come in for a minute?" he asks, soft and penitent.

She doesn't answer, just comes back down the hallway and waits for him. He closes the door, locks it, follows her tamely.

No no no. *Beat it*, she should have said. *Scram. Get out of here.*

"Do you want to give me your coat?" she asks.

He unbuttons it with slow red fingers. Raises eyebrows to me, which could mean anything or nothing. She hangs the coat next to mine in the closet and says matter-of-factly, "We were going to have dessert. Would you like some coffee?"

Humble nod.

Into the kitchen she goes, measures beans into the grinder, presses down on the lid. Screaming whine fills the house. Alan, clot of dried shaving blood on his jawline, never takes his eyes off her back. I've got to tell him about us, fast, before he gets down on his knees and begs her to take him back.

First, though, hand him a tissue for his dripping nose. Crust at the corners of his eyes: dried tears.

"Good thing you're here," he says, folding the tissue over on itself and using it again. "She might not have let me in otherwise."

Move closer, in case she's listening. "What are you doing here?"

"I made a wish that she would be home, even though I was sure she couldn't be. Good omen, right?"

Shit, to the Nth degree. "Hold on. Don't you remember what you said that night by the Christmas trees?"

He sees nothing but Lori, cutting slices of mocha cake for us. "What Christmas trees?"

"The night you walked out of the bar. You said you didn't belong with her."

"I don't remember that."

"You said, 'I can never make it up to her because we don't belong together.' "

Dabbing at his nostrils with the folded tissue, "I wasn't in my right mind that night. We *do* belong together. Maybe you could stick around tonight, help her get used to me again—old buddy old pal."

And looks me twinklingly in the eye, through the crust of tears.

I'VE GOT A PRICK OF MY OWN, YOU BLIND MAN. Or, since I can't say that, at least say this: "I'm sorry I didn't tell you before, I didn't want to hurt you when you were down. I've been going out with her since Halloween." Say more, don't leave it at that, an arrow through his throat. "I thought you were going to marry Suzanne."

His focus falls like a shot duck, down to my chest, down to the floor. A vein in his throat ticks. He can't accuse me—not after abandoning her, not after I ran in front of a car for him—but I have betrayed him nevertheless.

Here comes Lori with a silver tray, coffee and cake, forks and spoons, napkins in simple black rings. Their Royal Doulton wedding china, sugar and milk in matching gilt-edged pieces, pretentious and out of place amid the contemporary furnishings. If only I'd kissed her first and married her, before he buried her in all this *stuff.*

"Why are you still standing?" she asks us, and takes the end of the couch closest to the door.

I sit on the opposite couch-end, so as not to rub his nose in it. He eases down slowly into the leather-web chair, facing us across the coffee table. Or, not facing us: head turned toward the audio rack and the CD tower. Things he bought but no longer owns.

"Where are you living now?" she asks civilly, to punish him.

"Fort Greene. In my building. An empty apartment."

"Are you planning to stay there?"

"I'm not sure."

I could ask about his legal situation, give him a break from Lori's arctic freeze, but he might cry.

"How is your father's gall bladder?" Lori asks.

"He had it removed. He's better now."

"That's good. Is your mother still dating that podiatrist?"

"No, she ended it. She said he bored her."

"What about Carl and Margie, how are they?"

She could keep this up for as long as it takes to drive him away, but he says, "Everybody's great" and scratches the side of his jaw, and like the miraculous statue of a saint, he spouts blood. Unaware of the bright red drop trickling down his throat, he takes a sip of coffee and sets the cup down on the saucer. Lori walks off to the bathroom without explanation, startling him. I tap my own jaw, "You're bleeding."

Touches the place, sees the blood on his finger, stares at it dully. Can't use the linen napkin, so he goes to the kitchen for a paper towel. Wipes his throat, folds the towel, holds it against his jaw. Gazing into the pan with the lemon slices. Presumably, she used to make this dish for him, too.

Lori hands him a bandaid, and he uses the reflection in the microwave door to put it on. Rinses the blood off his hands, takes another paper towel to dry off, then follows

Lori back to the living room, to resume our pleasant little chat.
"You're going to hang your paintings?" he asks her.
"Burt has been telling me to for years."
"He's right, it's a good idea."
Tick of Lori's cup against saucer. Tick of mine. Alan watching her steadily, and therefore she won't look up from her coffee.
"Excuse me," she says, "I have to clean up."
Back to the kitchen she goes. Pours powder into the dishwasher's door and turns it on, though it's only half full. Efficient machine hum, barely audible.
Alan contemplating the dried flowers where *The Iliad* and *The Odyssey* used to be.
Turns to me. Studies my face, while blood darkens the bandaid.
"Do you think you'll marry her?" he asks.
Not sure whether he means, *If you think so, you're fooling yourself,* or simply, *What do you expect to happen?* Be cautious.
"Because if you're serious, if you really think she wants to be with you, I'll stay out of the way."
He's gazing at me forthrightly, with such dignity that I can't reply. I had forgotten, completely, his capacity for this kind of gesture.
He's waiting for an answer. Do I expect to marry her?
"I'm serious, but I can't say if it'll work out. It's been an awkward beginning. For obvious reasons."
He allows me time to add more. Behind him, Lori scours the bottom of the dinner-pan at the sink. What else could I say? The only thing I can think of is that I've never told Lori, *I love you.*
He stands, "I'm sorry, Burt," and goes into the kitchen. Which means I must follow, when really I'd rather curl up and go to sleep.
Lori, sharply, "I don't want to hear this."
Get in there.
"I know what I put you through," while she sets the wet

pan back on the stove and wipes down the already shining countertop. "It's eating me up. I want to come back and make you happy again—happier than we were before."

The dishwasher clunks into a new cycle, water sprays the inner walls. Chlorine scent. I have to say something, but can't think straight.

Unyielding Lori, "Go home, Alan. I don't want to hear how bad you feel."

Wet red eyes, "I love you more now than I ever did."

I've already become ridiculous, standing here this long without speaking. But that knowledge makes it even harder to begin.

Lori takes his love and mocks it. "I'm not the one you couldn't get out of your mind. Remember?"

"You *are*. I can't think of anything but how good you were to me."

There is one thing I can say. The truth. "You just want relief, Alan. You're forgetting how you really felt."

To Lori, not me, "I've been going over this in my mind for weeks. I see everything more clearly now than I ever have before. My judgment was distorted when I left. You have to understand, all these years, I've wondered if Suzanne was the—I was wrong, just wrong. But I had to spend time with her or I never would have known for sure."

"You can't kill something and then bring it back to life because you're sorry. Just go away."

"I can't—"

Not waiting for him to finish his sentence, she heads out of the room, but he reaches out and grabs her wrist, stops her, so I have no choice but to seize the arm that has seized hers—his knobby elbow in my grip, how weird—and now I can't let go until he does or I lose the contest (while all that's civilized in me says, *Let go, stop being a jerk*—but I must not listen, must for once acknowledge the deeper laws of the species, and fight for her to the finish), while blood seeps out from behind the bandaid, down his throat.

"Let go, Alan," I say. "Don't make this worse than it is."

I'm risking a fist in the nose, be ready for it—but all he

does is release Lori and shake my hand away, the way you shake off a bug. "I have to talk to you," he tells her. "Just give me ten minutes alone with you."

"Lori, go upstairs, let me talk to him."

She answers Alan, not me. There's a crack in her voice I've never heard before. "I don't *want* to talk to you. I want you to leave me alone."

"I won't go until you listen."

That's it. No more compassion. "Why should she listen to you when you don't listen to her? The whole world doesn't revolve around you and your monumental feelings."

By moving one of his feet three inches to the side, he solidifies his stance: a statue in the middle of the kitchen, immovable. He repeats, "Give me ten minutes."

Lori's chest lifts and falls slightly with each breath. She crosses past us, reaches into a drawer and takes out a long, black-handled knife—*No, this isn't possible*—picks up the zebra painting, pierces the middle of the canvas. Opens a gash up to the corner, then tosses the knife into the sink and drops the painting loudly on the floor, face down. Arms crossed, she leans back against the huge refrigerator and stares through the doorway, away from us and the painting, breathing through her nose quickly, shallowly.

The two edges of the gash curl away from each other, resembling a long thin mouth, closed and quiet after screaming, *She'll never feel this much for you.*

Alan, softly, "I'm sorry, but I can't go until I talk to you. I promise to leave after ten minutes."

Despairing half-laugh from Lori. "Now I'm irresistible. After all this time."

Implacable, tedious, "Ten minutes."

The dishwasher shifts into a steady hum. Lori turns to me, *Got anything to say?*

Yes, I do, but first must shake off the paralyzing sense that Alan wants her more than I do, needs her more than I do. "Lori, I know it's—I'm afraid you're going to let him stay, just out of kindness, and then he won't go away, he'll just wait you out until you lose the will to say No. But it doesn't have to happen that way."

The future depends on what I say in the next thirty seconds. This is my last chance to reach the center of her, to give her a reason to resist him.

"I think we could be happy together, I really do. But you have to give it time."

Mercy in her gaze, fondness but not love. The calm of surrender.

"I think I'd better just talk to him," she says. "Or he'll never leave."

Useless to keep fighting, then. Might as well hold onto my dignity. "I can wait upstairs."

"I don't think so. I just want go to to sleep. We can talk tomorrow."

"I'd really rather wait upstairs."

She won't look at me. "I can't—deal with this. Just let me..."

She's going to cry unless I let go. "Okay. I'll leave."

Alan stays in the kitchen while I collect my jacket, gloves, guitar. The air in the entranceway is full of garlic and lemon. Warm aroma of a life I'm not going to have.

No last words. Zip jacket, pull gloves on.

"Good night, Burt."

"Good night."

No kiss, no touch. She turns the key, opens the door, and I'm out, into the clear dry cold. Guitar in its case, unplayed, heavy in my hand. Close the gate behind me.

In the window, her white turtleneck above the sweatshirt. Empty face as she reaches for the wand: unhappy wife closing up the house for the night.

Christmas lights still up next door, green, red, blue, yellow. I could wait, see if he really leaves, on the off chance that I'm wrong and haven't lost her. Could run back and prove that I too have passion—but there's no point. She saw the difference between us: his ardor and my uncertainty. The matter is settled.

The walk to the subway, a post-break-up tradition.

Freezing wind blowing guitar case against my leg. Murmur in Elvis baritone, "That's the end of your sweetheart, that's the end of your friend..."

Stop. No need to sing about heartache.

No need to hurry home, either. What's there, that I need to rush back to? Nada. Nada thing. Therefore ignore the cold, take a stroll, see the world. (Breakup after breakup. I can't make these things last. What the hell is wrong with me?)

Beautiful slice of Manhattan skyline down this narrow street. Good location for a movie about 1850: red brick rowhouses, white sills underlining the windows. Lights on but shades drawn, except in one ground-floor window. Between white shutters, setting the table, a woman with long curls and hippie dress, an appealing crooked smile. Could write her a letter and put it in her box, addressed to Mystery Woman. *Walking down your street one sad, freezing night, I was cheered by the sight of you. If the enclosed picture doesn't repel you, call me.*

Goodbye, Lori. Goodbye, Alan. You have each other, and I have another chance to find someone to belong with. Someone of my own.

Epilogue

LAST NIGHT WHEN I came to bed, Patty asked what I want to do about a best man. I said, "Lament the absence of one?" She suggested George, but I only met him two years ago, first day in Gross Anatomy, and though I like him a lot, I don't think of him as a best friend. Asking him would be inappropriate, verging on pathetic.

"If you'd married me sooner," she said, "you could've had Alan."

"You were a lesbian then."

Punch in the shoulder, as if that were an obnoxious wisecrack, though I only meant it as fact.

"I can't believe you're really resigned to having no close friends. Unless refusing to have a best man is a cry for help."

"I don't have time for friends right now. I hardly have time for you."

"That's true."

She went on to warn me against turning into a solitary old father-in-the-corner, hiding behind my newspaper while boisterous family life goes on around me. We sparred pleasantly on that topic, but my mind was elsewhere. Specifically:

Last month, during my clerkship in surgery, a college student had a cancerous testicle removed. While he was in the recovery room, I saw a guy and girl in the lounge down the hall, both in torn-knee jeans, both staring grimly at the Monet poster opposite. Roommate and girlfriend, I assumed. Something in the scene had a familiar tone, which took a few minutes to pinpoint: they looked like Lori and I would have if Alan had gone through cancer surgery when we were 21.

I hadn't missed him once in the five years since he took his wife back from me, but seeing the young pair in the lounge made me wince with nostalgic yearning. I wished I could sweep everything aside and have him back as my friend. Memories have been going off in my head like flashbulbs ever since. The New Year's Eve in Times Square, us crushed against the stoned girl with a lit cigarette held above her head, which she almost stuck in Alan's ear except that I grabbed her wrist, to which she mumbled, "You're so tough." Sophomore year, an hour before my date with the bosomy cellist Darlene Ziegelbaum, when he showed me (just in case I lost my virginity that night) how to excite a woman before sex with your finger. *The Deer Hunter* at the lecture hall, both of us crying—Alan out loud, me silently—because Robert DeNiro went back to Viet Nam to rescue his friend Christopher Walken and found him just in time to see him die. The three days he stayed with me after his Seventh Avenue suicide walk, and we ate dinner together and talked for hours, about his business and our families and growing up, and by the time he left, *I* was the one who dreaded coming home to an empty apartment.

All of which raises the question, Should I invite them to the wedding?

Put it this way: I want to, despite everything. I ran into Ugly during my obstetrics rotation, bringing his wife in for an amnio, and he told me that Alan has a baby now, a million dollar house in Short Hills, and a Mercedes. He ticked off these belongings boastfully, as if they were his, while I shuddered, wondering what Alan has become. He also reported that Alan had to do community service for a while because of some business problem, but his lawyer found him a women's shelter that needed accounting help, and he got off painlessly.

I want to see him, if only to know what to think about him.

"*Ayyyy.*"

Mrs. Fernandez, pneumonia and phlebitis. A sigh, and she stops. I should finish writing up the admissions and go home, but there's one more problem to think through: Lori. Can't have Alan at the wedding without having her too. That Sunday morning on the phone, *I've never stopped thinking about him*—which I can't forgive, even though I already knew.

So, the big question. Do I wish I could have married her instead of Patty?

Maybe—if she could have loved me. If frogs could fly. (Because with Patty everything has been so calm and sensible. Since the day she kissed me on the bench by the river, that is, and confessed that she wasn't strictly, exclusively gay, and I had the intoxicating pleasure of learning that the woman I most admired had wanted me all along. But since then it's been so comfortable, so devoid of obstacles, of thwarted and inflamed desire. No more loneliness, but no more thrills.)

Brisk, heavy footsteps, shoes not slippers, i.e., staff not patient. Who is it, and let's hope he doesn't want anything from me.

Marvin Borg, loathsome intern, lousy posture, never smiles. "I need help with a sepsis workup. Satchmo just spiked a fever."

Half past midnight, I should be home in bed by now, but a third-year student doesn't refuse an intern.

Patients shifting in their beds as we pass, a polka on someone's quiet radio, fluorescent lights that make even the walls look ill. Flavia the nurse eating sesame noodles at her station. Ordinary night at the hospital, nothing glamorous or inspiring in sight—is this the goal I've worked my ass off to reach?—yet, a solid satisfaction that I've made it, I'm here, I did what I wanted to do.

"You know Satchmo's history, right?"

Robot voice, it's all I can do to keep from mimicking. "He's a chauffeur. He had an emergency hemodialysis today."

"They put him on a restricted sodium diet and his wife finds him unconscious with a bag of potato chips in his hand." Flicker of a sneer, *These people.* "Cardiac failure, chronic renal failure, a stroke, and now this."

Satchmo is sweating heavily, nodding to himself. (He looks nothing like Louie Armstrong, just the bug eyes.)

"Good evening, Mr. Young, how are we doing this evening?"
Not pleased to see us. "More needles?"
"I'm afraid so."
Borg's impersonation of a human being is unconvincing. Satchmo, meanwhile, out at sea in a leaky boat, has no small talk in him.
"We're going to try to see what's causing your fever," I tell him, just so he knows.
"Huh," not listening, but then he changes, looks into my face. "Damn foolish, winding up in the hospital 'cause of potato chips."
"You couldn't eat just one?"
Steely little grimace of a smile. He gets the joke.
It's late, that's enough talk. While the intern draws the old man's blood, I remember Alan, how before he would eat potato chips, he used to spread them on paper napkins to draw off at least a fraction of the oil.
All right. I'll invite him to the wedding. He'll probably invent an excuse (the baby has a horseback riding lesson) and put an enthusiastic *Congratulations!* on the RSVP, and that will be that.
(But what if they come?)

•

3:07 A.M.
"Patty Cake?"
Out cold. Not with her usual scrunched-against-the-pillow sleep-frown but on her back, mouth open, as if she dropped here in exhaustion and lost consciousness before she could turn over. Olive eye-shadow still on, flecks of baby's breath in her hair. *My wife.* How strange. I'm married now. A husband.
Just finished wrapping the top tier of the cake in foil and a baggie, stowed in the freezer to be eaten on our first anniversary. (My mother said we had to, it's a custom.) One rented tux shoe lies in the corner on its side. Out in the liv-

ing room, through the doorway, a mountain of wrapped boxes and a pile of envelopes on the table. Though we needed nothing, we've been given so much.

Wiped out, but not ready to close my eyes. I want to bring it all back, to preserve as much as I can before it drifts further into the ghostly past. We were royalty tonight. A hundred people came to make us happy, and in lifting us, they lifted themselves as well.

Was it? Yes it was, the happiest day of my life. Completely unexpected—thought I'd hate being the object of gawking. (Just before the ceremony, told George my theory about weddings, that the village requires a human sacrifice from time to time and today it's me.) But instead of disliking the attention, we basked in it, and carried ourselves with a grace I didn't know either of us had. "You look so good," different people said, and for once I was able to enjoy the compliments instead of batting them away.

So many beautiful moments, the kind that won't show up in photos but that I'll remember forever. Stern, unsentimental Patty in her sister's wedding dress, her hoarse voice cracking as she recited her vow, "I want to wake up beside you every morning for the rest of my life"—the crack in the voice outweighing all of my doubts. I held her hand so tight that the new ring hurt her; "You're breaking my finger," she whispered. And the ring: wiggling it with my thumb, the shine and the awkward feeling, too perfectly round for my finger. And Uncle Gunther, first time I've seen him since my father's funeral—his face a thinner version of my father's, constricted with the same emotion that contorted mine as we shook hands, each seeing my father again in the other's face. And the table of college friends teasing me about all the blind dates they set me up on, with cousins, neighbors, co-workers, and I got to tell one more time the old story of Terry the correction officer and the gun in her panty-drawer. Even Rhonda and Charlie, usually at each others' throats, slow-dancing tenderly as if this night had the power to heal wounds. And clumsy, bearish George, dancing tipsily by himself, giving me a big shirt-hanging-out hug, and ending up in the corner of a couch, snoring. And Alan—the surge of blood when he walked in. I was helping the rabbi carry a little table up the aisle, and had about twelve other tasks to do before the ceremony could begin, and my busy distractedness left room for only simple emotions, in this case exhilaration. I set down the table and strode back down the aisle—Alan and Lori peering around self-consciously, like people who come to a party where they know no one—and then the gladness in our mutually tight grip, him in an olive summer suit, looking smaller (the heels on my tux shoes, I realize now) but no older, and Lori just behind him with a warm small smile, not at all confident that my good will included her, but there was so much loveliness and consideration in that face, all I could do was let go of my stale grudge and wish her well. "Congratulations, it's great to see you," "Thanks, how are you both doing?" "Great," "You look terrific," "*You* do—that tux!" "Thanks for inviting us," "I'm really glad you came"—so much emotion imprisoned in such ordinary words, and then I had to leave them and finish setting up, as someone yelled, "Schwarzkopf!"

I saw them again after the ceremony, in the cocktail hour, Alan telling a story to a loud circle of college friends as I brought Patty over. Charlie made us recount the tale of our recent moving day, when the City Marshall almost towed the truck with all our belongings on it because the movers hadn't paid their parking tickets; hearty laughter from one and all, as if we were their king and queen. Then Patty had to go help her aunt find the silver kiddush cup, which the aunt had borrowed from her temple, and Alan said in my ear, "She's perfect for you, I'm really happy for you," while Lori nodded in agreement, both wanting me to believe that I was better off with Patty than I would have been with Lori. One thing that bothered me was Alan's manicured fingernails—noticed only later, as Patty and I made the rounds during dessert—but just as I spotted them, the band came back from their dinner and broke into an over-amplified "Hava Nagila." Patty said, "Huh?" because we never asked for this ethnic kitsch (my mother paid them off, we found out later) but then someone pulled us into the ragged, growing circle and around we went, fifty people doing fifty versions of the archaic folkdance, Uncle Morris' sweaty hand in mine. I kicked self-consciously, because what did this Yiddishkeit have to do with me? But then I saw my mother's white teeth flashing from her California tan, a rare sight, and even Aunt Rose who complained about having to climb three flights of stairs squawked in delight, even skeptical Patty (in jeans because she could only tolerate the wedding dress for so long) kicking her feet along with everybody else, both of us learning to enjoy the dance, and then my shul-going cousins swept us up on chairs—"Hold onto the seat," I called to Patty, remembering the story of the bride who fell and was paralyzed for life (never thought I would someday ride four men's shoulders, a regular Motel Kamzoil)—but it was gratifying to see Alan down there on the right front chairleg, drunk and giddy, as if he had found a way back to freshman year, ecstatically lifting me above the crowd. The chair business ended sooner than I wanted it to, and we took our places in the circle again, the band playing "L'Chaim" now, not letting us stop even though the dance had lost its novelty, around and around, everyone waiting for something new to happen, and then Alan came over from across the circle, half-blind with liquor by now, and dragged me into the center. When I was ten and saw men dancing the kazatsky at a cousin's wedding, I fervently aspired to do the same someday, but after the bicycle accident, unable to bend my knee all the way, I resigned myself to the idea of watching other men dance the kazatsky at my wedding—yet here I was with Alan, my hands gripped tight by his, kicking out with alternating legs, the bad knee warning me not to bend any further, but the clapping all around and the ancestral music and Alan pulling me downward—all drove me to forget caution, and I went down almost to the floor, lower than I thought I could, the guests cheering and whistling, my wooden heels rapping the floorboards, Alan panting but not slowing down, the band playing "Sholom Aleichem" now, and I felt myself growing, expanding with pleasure, until Alan yanked me up and let go of my hands—*no, not yet*—only to grab them again with crossed arms, and this time there were no special steps, only quick-footed turning, around and around in a circle of two, toes almost touching as centrifugal force pulled our shoulders in opposite directions, but his damp hands gripped my wrists like handcuffs, and mine held his, and all the other faces blurred behind the one clear face as we went faster, challenging each other, keeping each other from falling, savoring it with pounding heart—Alan's eyes squinted down to dark slits—and the wounds of the past were washed clean, we were best friends again, for one night at least, and even though my chest ached from dancing so hard, for once in my life I could feel a joy this big, as big as the circle of family and friends—panting, almost gasping, pulled apart by our turning but holding each other in the double handshake, and that's why everyone was clapping, to see the old friends together again—heart pounding painfully, but not wanting to stop—dizzyingly fast, dangerously fast—holding on to each other as tight as we could.